Chronicles of Suborno Deb Barman

Mysteries of Stolen Memory

Aurobindo Ghosh

Ukiyoto Publishing

All global publishing rights are held by

Ukiyoto Publishing

Published in 2024

Content Copyright © Aurobindo Ghosh

ISBN 9789367959886

All rights reserved.
No part of this publication may be reproduced, transmitted, or stored in a retrieval system, in any form by any means, electronic, mechanical, photocopying, recording or otherwise, without the prior permission of the publisher.

The moral rights of the author have been asserted.

This is a work of fiction. Names, characters, businesses, places, events, locales, and incidents are either the products of the author's imagination or used in a fictitious manner. Any resemblance to actual persons, living or dead, or actual events is purely coincidental.

This book is sold subject to the condition that it shall not by way of trade or otherwise, be lent, resold, hired out or otherwise circulated, without the publisher's prior consent, in any form of binding or cover other than that in which it is published.

www.ukiyoto.com

I dedicate this book to my loving niece Sushmita Roy (Mishtu), her ever smiling husband Abhyuday Roy (Joy) and their little fairy Aahana Roy (Pihu).

My heartfelt gratitude goes to my wife, Dr. Sharada Ghosh, whose discerning eye and unwavering commitment to excellence have been invaluable to this book. As a dedicated critic and meticulous editor, she has not only identified every flaw but has also painstakingly worked to make each story flow seamlessly. Her tireless efforts in editing, compiling, and organizing these narratives have been essential to this work.

I am also profoundly grateful to my children Dr. Dorothy, Dr. Gargi, and Aalap who form the foundation of my support system. Their encouragement and faith in my writing give me the strength to pursue this passion. To each of you, thank you for your patience, understanding, and belief in me.

Lastly, let me take this opportunity to convey my gratitude to all the team members of Ukiyoto publishing for their maximum care to make this book a magnificent creation.

Contents

Preface   1

Part One   7

Chapter One - The Launch of the book 'Mysteries of Our
Brain'   8
Chapter Two - Dr. Aryan Kapoor's Laboratory and the
Mysteries of the Brain   17
Chapter Three - Neural Plasticity with Fuzzy Logic   32
Chapter Four - The Science of Memory and Neural
Connections   38
Chapter Five - The Science of Hypnotism – A
Neuroscientific Approach   46
Chapter Six - Concept of Neuroengineering   55
Chapter Seven - Somesh the Healer   68
Chapter Eight - Malicious Ambition   75
Chapter Nine - Mysterious Emails   83
Chapter Ten - The Meeting   101
Chapter Eleven - Mysterious Disappearance   114
Chapter Twelve - The truth   121
Chapter Thirteen - The Clue   126
Chapter Fourteen - International linkage   130
Chapter Fifteen - Back in India   135

Part Two   138

Chapter Sixteen - Somewhere in southern India   139
Chapter Seventeen - The brewing of doubt   145
Chapter Eighteen - Anticipation of the Project Mnemosyne
                                                                    151
Chapter Nineteen - Lab goes down   155
Chapter Twenty - Alarm Bell calling   161
Chapter Twenty One - A Visitor   164
Chapter Twenty Two - Lure and Plan   170

Chapter Twenty Three - Breakthrough   176
Chapter Twenty Four - Semi-Incarnation   182
Chapter Twenty Five - Breach and Treachery   190
Chapter Twenty Six - The Setup: Preparing the Net   204

About the Author   *220*

Foreword

It is rare to encounter an individual who excels in such a diverse range of fields with as much passion and dedication as Dr Ghosh. An academician with two PhDs, he has spent almost four decades shaping minds as a teacher, guide, and motivational speaker. Beyond his professional achievements, Dr Ghosh is a multi-faceted personality with a deep-rooted interest in traditional Indian art, a field he pursues alongside his writing career. Over the years, he has penned numerous books, ranging from profound philosophical explorations of the Upanishads to captivating works of fiction. His writings have reached a wide audience, with translations into multiple languages, reflecting his commitment to bridging cultural divides. As a linguist, he has written in several languages, including his mother tongue, Bengali.

Away from the public spotlight, Dr Ghosh has been engaged in the monumental task of restoring his ancestral 'haveli,' a heritage property that has stood for over five centuries in Champanagar, located in the suburbs of Bhagalpur, Bihar. This place holds historical significance, with references dating back to the period of the Mahabharata when it was known as 'Angaa.' This deep connection to heritage, culture, and history is one of the many layers that shape Dr Ghosh's unique perspective.

I have had the privilege of knowing Dr Ghosh since my childhood, and I have always been fascinated by his relentless pursuit of excellence in so many areas of life. His insatiable curiosity and sharp observational skills are reflected not only in his academic work but also in his art and writings. Dr Ghosh's approach to life is one of holistic engagement, seeking to understand and connect diverse elements of human existence. This is evident in his paintings as well as in the numerous books he has authored over the years, each reflecting his deep insights into both the human condition and the world around us.

His latest book, *Mysteries of Our Brain*, takes the reader on a journey into the cutting-edge field of neuroscience, exploring the complex relationship between the body and mind. In this thrilling narrative, Dr Ghosh introduces us to Dr Kapoor, a neuro-scientist on the verge of a revolutionary breakthrough in brain research. Dr Kapoor's research into restoring memories beyond the death and decay of brain cells holds the potential to reshape humanity's understanding of consciousness itself. However, this technological breakthrough also harbours dark implications. The ability to preserve memories indefinitely, or to transport them across time, could alter the very fabric of human evolution, with unintended consequences. A group of nefarious forces, led by a hypnotist, seeks to exploit Dr Kapoor's work for their own sinister purposes, forcing him into a high-stakes battle for survival and control over the future of humanity.

As the plot unfolds, Dr Ghosh deftly weaves together themes of science, mysticism, and international espionage. His brilliantly crafted detective, Suborno Deb Burman, is tasked with unravelling the conspiracy and rescuing Dr. Kapoor. In this fast-paced narrative, the reader is taken into a world of corporate greed, political intrigue, and the ethical dilemmas that arise from technological advancements that threaten to tip the balance of power. The stakes could not be higher, as the potential for this new technology to change the global order hangs in the balance.

In an era where attention spans are increasingly fragmented and the influence of social media constantly pulls at our focus, this book offers a gripping narrative that holds the reader's attention from start to finish. The questions raised by Dr Ghosh about the nature of memory, consciousness, and the soul's journey across different lifetimes are thought-provoking and timely. With neural chips already undergoing clinical testing and the concept of memory retention becoming a reality, *Mysteries of Our Brain* forces us to confront a future where the very essence of what it means to be human may be up for debate.

Dr Ghosh's exploration of these profound themes is not only a compelling work of fiction but also a thought experiment that challenges our perceptions of the mind, body, and soul. His writing delves into the consequences of technological advancements that promise to change the trajectory of human existence, offering a cautionary tale about the ethical and moral implications of wielding such power.

In this book, Dr Ghosh provides a vivid portrayal of a world on the brink of monumental change. The interplay of science and mysticism, the fight for control over ground-breaking technologies, and the looming threat of dystopian outcomes create a thrilling, yet deeply reflective narrative. It is a work that invites readers to question the future of humanity and to consider the implications of tampering with the very building blocks of consciousness itself.

I am certain that readers will find *Mysteries of Our Brain* to be both an intellectually stimulating and emotionally gripping experience. Dr. Ghosh's ability to blend complex scientific concepts with a captivating storyline makes this book a truly unique contribution to contemporary literature. It is a must-read for anyone who is curious about the future of neuroscience, memory, and the human mind.

Amit Sinha, CXO, Sector Specialist

Banking Financial Services and Insurance (BFSI)

Preface

The human brain, a marvel of biological engineering, remains the ultimate frontier in scientific exploration. Encased in its protective skull, it orchestrates our every thought, memory, and action, weaving the tapestry of human experience. 'Mysteries of Our Brain' by Dr. Aryan Kapoor is not just a book it is an odyssey into this fascinating and enigmatic organ. It ventures where few dare tread, decoding the language of neurons and the mysteries of memory, and offering insights that could redefine the boundaries of human potential. But with all great discoveries, the revelations within this book are a double-edged sword, bearing the potential for both healing and destruction.

Dr. Kapoor's journey began decades ago as a young neurosurgeon, driven by the desire to understand the intricacies of memory formation and retrieval. His groundbreaking research into neuro-engineering and memory preservation has opened a new realm of possibilities for medicine, offering solutions to conditions like Alzheimer's, trauma-induced amnesia, and cognitive decline. His work is hailed as a scientific milestone, holding the promise of transforming millions of lives. Yet, as the book takes readers through these profound discoveries, it also sounds an implicit warning about the perils of unbridled scientific advancement.

In a world where knowledge is power, the very breakthroughs that promise liberation can also be weaponized. Within the pages of Mysteries of Our Brain lies a chilling possibility: what if memory could be manipulated, controlled, or even erased? The implications are staggering, and the specter of such misuse looms large over Dr. Kapoor's work.

At the heart of this book lies the tension between scientific ambition and ethical responsibility. The research unveiled here has the power to unlock the deepest recesses of the human mind. It can help restore lost memories, enhance cognitive abilities, and even transfer knowledge from one brain to another. Yet, this same knowledge, if wielded by those with nefarious intent, could destabilize societies and compromise national security. The concept of weaponized memory manipulation is no longer a trope of science fiction; it is a potential reality that this book forces us to confront.

A Dark Horizon

In the wrong hands, Dr. Kapoor's research could herald an era of unprecedented control over human consciousness. Imagine a world where individuals are stripped of their memories and programmed with false narratives. Soldiers could be turned into unthinking automatons, and dissent could be crushed by erasing the very idea of rebellion. Governments could manipulate public opinion not through propaganda but by altering memories themselves. Such a dystopian scenario is no longer a distant fantasy but a plausible outcome if this research is exploited without checks and balances.

The stakes are particularly high given the current geopolitical landscape. As Mysteries of Our Brain reveals, several global powers are already racing to harness the potential of neuro-engineering for strategic advantage. The Chinese defense ministry, in particular, is rumored to view Dr. Kapoor's work as the key to developing mind-control technologies. This chilling prospect raises urgent ethical and policy questions: Should the pursuit of scientific knowledge take precedence over its potential misuse? How can society protect itself against the dark underbelly of such advancements?

The Responsibility of Knowledge

Dr. Kapoor's intent in publishing this book was clear: to democratize access to knowledge and spark a global conversation about the responsibilities that come with it. By making his findings accessible to a broader audience, he hoped to foster a shared understanding of the human brain and its infinite possibilities. However, he was acutely aware of the risks involved. Even as the book was being written, Kapoor confided in trusted colleagues about his fears of espionage and intellectual theft.

The narrative in Mysteries of Our Brain does not shy away from these concerns. Instead, it embraces them, providing readers with a nuanced view of both the promises and perils of neuro-engineering. Kapoor's research raises profound ethical dilemmas that will resonate with scientists, policymakers, and the general public alike. What safeguards can be put in place to ensure that such discoveries serve humanity rather than harm it? How can we strike a balance between innovation and regulation?

A Call to Vigilance

As readers delve into the pages of this book, they will encounter not only the marvels of neuroscience but also the dark possibilities that arise when science is divorced from ethics. The story of Mysteries of Our Brain serves as a wake-up call, urging society to remain vigilant about the dual-edged nature of scientific progress. It challenges us to consider the broader implications of our quest for knowledge and to recognize that with great power comes great responsibility.

The disappearance of Dr. Kapoor, detailed in the narrative surrounding this book, underscores the urgency of these issues. His abduction, linked to a covert operation by foreign agents, reveals the lengths to which some will go to exploit scientific breakthroughs for strategic gain. Detective Suborno Deb Barman's involvement in the investigation adds a layer of intrigue, but it also highlights the real-world dangers that accompany the pursuit of advanced knowledge.

Hope amidst Uncertainty

Despite these dangers, Mysteries of Our Brain is ultimately a testament to the resilience and ingenuity of the human spirit. Kapoor's research, while fraught with risks, also holds immense potential for good. It can unlock new treatments for debilitating conditions, enhance our understanding of the human mind, and inspire future generations of scientists to push the boundaries of what is possible.

The book invites readers to join a global dialogue about the future of neuroscience and its impact on society. It calls on policymakers to establish ethical frameworks for scientific research and on citizens to demand transparency and accountability from those who wield such knowledge. Most importantly, it reminds us that science, at its best, is a force for good a tool for understanding ourselves and improving the world we inhabit.

As you turn the pages of Mysteries of Our Brain, prepare to be enthralled by the wonders of neuroscience and the gripping story of its discovery. But also take a moment to reflect on the broader implications of this knowledge. What kind of world do we want to build with the insights gleaned from the human brain? How can we ensure that the power of science is used responsibly and equitably?

These are the questions that lie at the heart of Dr. Aryan Kapoor's work. They are questions that demand answers not just from scientists but from all of us. For in the end, the mysteries of our brain are not just about the organ itself they are about what it means to be human and the choices we make as we stand on the precipice of a new era in human history.

Part One

Chapter One - The Launch of the book 'Mysteries of Our Brain'

The town hall of Chandigarh was abuzz with excitement as people filled its aisles, eager to witness the grand launch of 'Mysteries of Our Brain', Dr. Aryan Kapoor's latest book. His contributions to neuroscience had already earned him accolades worldwide, and his recent foray into making complex brain science accessible to the public had struck a chord with both laypeople and professionals alike. Doctors, students, and even curious citizens from different parts of the region had gathered, ready to hear from the celebrated doctor himself.

The stage was set with an elegant backdrop bearing the title of the book in bold, sleek letters, beneath which the tagline read: "An exploration of the deepest secrets of the human mind." At one end of the stage sat Dr. Kapoor, visibly pleased and humbled by the gathering, flanked by three eminent neuroscientists invited to speak on the significance of his work. The publisher, seated nearby, occasionally scanned the room, taking the vibrant energy.

The evening began with an introductory speech by the host, who briefly recounted Dr. Kapoor's journey as a neurosurgeon, researcher, and now, an author. Applause filled the hall as Dr. Kapoor stood to greet the audience, his smile radiating warmth and humility. He took his seat, and the event commenced with the publisher announcing an exclusive 10% discount for anyone who booked a copy on the spot, as well as the chance to have their copies signed by Dr. Kapoor himself.

Dr. Aryan Kapoor's Speech

"Good evening, distinguished guests, colleagues, and curious minds.

It is a privilege to stand here before you as we celebrate not just the launch of a book but the dissemination of ideas that challenge, inspire, and push the boundaries of what we know about the human brain.

As a neurosurgeon and researcher, my work has always revolved around uncovering the mysteries of the brain—this organ that holds the secrets to our thoughts, emotions, and very identities. Through Mysteries of Our Brain, I sought to present groundbreaking discoveries in neuroscience in a way that is both accessible and thought-provoking. Allow me to briefly share some of the pioneering insights that the book explores.

Firstly, one of the most exciting frontiers in neuroscience today is our growing understanding of neuroplasticity that is the brain's remarkable ability to rewire itself. Traditionally, we believed that the adult brain was relatively fixed. However, recent research reveals that even in later life, our brains can adapt to injury, learn new skills, and form new connections. This insight opens avenues for therapies in stroke recovery, degenerative diseases, and mental health, offering hope where once there was none.

Secondly, the book delves into our exploration of the gut-brain axis. Emerging evidence shows that the micro biome in our gut plays a significant role in shaping our mental health and cognitive abilities. This bidirectional relationship between our gut and brain is revolutionizing how we approach disorders like anxiety, depression, and even neurodegenerative conditions.

Another cornerstone of the book is the breakthrough in decoding neural signals using advanced neuroimaging and AI. These tools allow us to visualize brain activity in unprecedented detail, enabling early diagnosis of diseases like Alzheimer's and even translating thought patterns into actionable data. Imagine a world where someone paralyzed by disease can communicate using just their thoughts—what seemed like science fiction is now within reach.

Lastly, Mysteries of Our Brain examines the ethics of these advancements. As we gain the power to manipulate memory, alter behavior, or even augment intelligence, how do we ensure these technologies serve humanity responsibly?

This book is a culmination of years of work, collaboration, and reflection. It aims to inspire readers to not only understand their brains better but also to appreciate the profound implications of these discoveries on our lives.

Thank you for being part of this journey. I hope this book sparks the same awe and curiosity in you that drive our research every day.

Thank you."

After the announcement, the first guest speaker, Dr. Meera Arora, a renowned neurology professor, took the stage. Her years of research and teaching made her words impactful as she spoke with conviction about the importance of Dr. Kapoor's work.

Dr. Meera Arora's Speech

"Good evening everyone! It is a true privilege to stand here today in the honor of Dr. Kapoor's remarkable achievement. 'Mysteries of Our Brain' is not only a book but a guide, a key, that opens doors to the marvels of the human brain, the organ that defines our thoughts, our emotions, our memories, and ultimately, our lives.

As a professor of neurology, I have long been aware of Dr. Kapoor's work in both neurosurgery and brain research. His contributions in memory restoration have given countless people a second chance of living a fuller life, freeing them from the shackles of lost memories. But what makes 'Mysteries of Our Brain' truly unique is Dr. Kapoor's ability to translate his profound scientific knowledge into concepts accessible to all. He does this with clarity, without diluting the richness of the subject.

For those who are not neuroscientists, this book will shed light on the sheer power of your own brain; how it works, how it remembers, and how it heals. To those of us who work in this field, this book is a bridge between clinical practice and everyday life, helping us reconnect with the very human side of our work. This is why I am proud to recommend 'Mysteries of Our Brain' as essential reading, not only for experts but for everyone who wants to understand the incredible potential we all carry within us. Thank you, Dr. Kapoor, for sharing your knowledge with the world."

Applause echoed through the hall as Dr. Kapoor finished her speech, and a visible sense of excitement filled the air. The next speaker was Dr. Amarjit Singh, a pioneering neurosurgeon with decades of experience in brain surgery and rehabilitation.

The second guest speaker Neuro-surgeon Dr. Amarjit Singh's Speech

"Thank you, Dr. Kapoor, and thank you, for inviting me to speak at this incredible event. I have had the pleasure of knowing Dr. Kapoor professionally for several years, and I can say without hesitation that he has raised the bar in our field. What you hold in your hands today is more than just a book; it's a comprehensive guide to the neural landscapes that define human existence.

In our day-to-day medical practice, especially in surgery, we often become so focused on the physical aspects of our work, the precision, and the techniques, that we lose sight of the profound psychological and emotional dimensions. 'Mysteries of Our Brain' takes us beyond the anatomy of the brain. Dr. Kapoor delves into how memories are formed, stored, and sometimes lost. His insights into the processes drive cognitive functions and emotions allow us to see the brain not just as a network of cells, but as the seat of the soul.

As a surgeon, I am particularly fascinated by Dr. Kapoor's work on memory restoration. His detailed chapters on memory pathways and neural plasticity, how the brain can rewire itself after trauma; are invaluable to practitioners like myself who deal with patients affected by traumatic brain injuries. He gives us not only scientific explanations but also an ethical perspective on the responsibilities we hold as caretakers of this knowledge. I urge everyone here to read this book and see for yourself the beauty and intricacies of your mind."

The hall resounded with another round of applause as Dr. Singh took his seat. His words had touched many, especially the students and young doctors in attendance. The final speaker of the evening was Dr. Nikhil Sharma, a neuropsychologist who specialized in hypnosis and memory studies; a subject Dr. Kapoor had explored extensively in his book.

The third guest speaker renowned neurologist Dr. Nikhil Sharma's Speech

"Ladies and gentlemen, it's a pleasure to join you all this evening to celebrate the launch of Dr. Kapoor's masterful work, 'Mysteries of Our Brain'. I must say, I was both inspired and impressed when I read it, and I feel privileged to share my thoughts with you today.

Dr. Kapoor has done something extraordinary with this book: he has taken the mysterious and, frankly, intimidating world of neuroscience and made it relatable, digestible, and fascinating for everyone. One of the key aspects that struck me was his approach to memory and hypnotism. Hypnosis, a tool that can sometimes seem shrouded in mystery, is explained here with the scientific rigor it deserves. He explores how hypnosis can serve as a therapeutic method for memory retrieval and how it works by activating specific parts of the brain, notably the prefrontal cortex and hippocampus.

Dr. Kapoor also shares compelling insights into memory disorders and age-related cognitive decline, highlighting the urgent need for research in these areas. In doing so, he not only educates the public but also sends a clear message to the scientific community: the study of the brain should extend beyond pathology. It should include the discovery of methods to enhance mental resilience, improve memory function, and perhaps even uncover ways to store memories safely.

In a time when mental health is finally beginning to receive the attention it deserves, 'Mysteries of Our Brain' provides a roadmap for both professionals and laypeople to understand, respect, and protect the brain's remarkable capabilities. Dr. Kapoor, thank you for this wonderful gift to the humanity."

As Dr. Sharma finished his speech, the audience erupted in applause, many visibly moved by his words. Each of the three speakers had touched on different aspects of Dr. Kapoor's work, underscoring the wide-reaching impact of his book.

Book Signing and Conclusion of the Ceremony

The ceremony continued with Dr. Kapoor signing copies of his book. A long line formed, each attendee clutching their newly purchased copies, eager to have them signed. Many thanked him personally, sharing how his book had already influenced their perspectives or sparked their curiosity. The publisher stood nearby, delighted with the response, as people continued to book additional copies to share with friends and family.

When Dr. Kapoor finally completed the book signing, the publisher thanked everyone and reminded the audience of the on-the-spot discount, which many continued to take advantage of that. Attendees left the town hall that evening with a new sense of wonder about the mysteries of the brain, feeling as though they had taken a small yet profound step into a world of uncharted mental landscapes.

Was it correct to launch a book of this magnitude of scientific research and let it go to the general public without screening?

As Dr. Kapoor left the venue, he knew that his journey with 'Mysteries of Our Brain' was just beginning.

Through this book, his knowledge was no longer confined to the walls of a lab or a lecture hall; it was now out in the world, in the hands of people from all walks of life. His hope was that it would serve not only as an educational tool but also as an inspiration a reminder of the incredible potential that resides within each and every mind. None expected the book to become number one bestselling book not only in India but abroad too.

Chapter Two - Dr. Aryan Kapoor's Laboratory and the Mysteries of the Brain

1. The Laboratory of Dr. Aryan Kapoor

In a city known for its blend of historic architecture and cutting-edge technology, hidden in the high-rise skyline, stands a modern fortress of science. This is the Neurosciences and Neurotechnology Lab, the research domain of Dr. Aryan Kapoor. Within its walls, every corner, every wire, and every piece of equipment speaks of a dedication to unraveling the most complex organ known to humankind—the human brain.

Dr. Kapoor's lab is unlike any traditional medical laboratory. It is an expansive, meticulously designed space combining elements of a neurosurgical theater, a research facility, and a futuristic command center. An entire wall is covered with large, interactive screens showing live data from patients and research subjects around the world. A dozen computer terminals are linked to the lab's high-powered servers, which run algorithms to analyze neural data in real-time.

Along the lab's perimeter stand a series of workstations, each equipped with high-resolution microscopes, slides containing samples of neural tissues, and devices for measuring neuronal activity. At the center is a state-of-the-art holographic projection system, capable of displaying 3D models of brain structures in fine detail. It allows Dr. Kapoor and his team to "walk through" the brain, examining structures down to the individual neuron level.

In a separate, soundproofed wing of the lab, patients recline in advanced neural interfaces, their heads fitted with non-invasive EEG caps. These devices use an array of sensors to capture even the faintest electromagnetic signals emitted by the brain. Here, Dr. Kapoor conducts his experiments on memory, cognition, and neuroplasticity, closely studying how specific neurons light up during memory recall or decision-making.

2. From Dr. Kapoor's Note book

The Human Brain:

An In-Depth Exploration of Neurological Structure and Function of brain and some technical explanation required before the discussion of main research of Dr. Kapoor

a) Neuroscience

- Definition: Neuroscience is the scientific study of the nervous system, particularly the brain and spinal cord. This field examines how the brain and nervous system function, how they impact behavior, and how they can be influenced by genetics, environment, and experience.

- Relevance in Dr. Kapoor's Work: As the backbone of his research, neuroscience provides Dr. Kapoor with insights into how complex networks of neurons form connections, store memories, and influence various functions like cognition, emotions, and behavior. His understanding of neuroscience forms the basis of his approach to conditions like memory loss, neural plasticity, and brain injury.

b) Neurosurgeon

- Definition: A neurosurgeon is a medical doctor specialized in diagnosing and treating disorders of the brain, spinal cord, and nerves through surgery. They treat conditions such as brain tumors, spinal cord injuries, and neurological disorders.

- Dr. Kapoor's Role as a Neurosurgeon: Before becoming a renowned Neurophysicist, Dr. Kapoor was a celebrated neurosurgeon who treated thousands of patients suffering from various neurological conditions, including memory loss and brain trauma. His experience as a neurosurgeon gave him a practical, hands-on understanding of brain anatomy and neural pathways.

c) Neuroplasticity

- Definition: Neuroplasticity, or brain plasticity, is the brain's ability to reorganize and form new neural connections throughout life. It allows the brain to adapt to changes, recover from injury, and acquire new skills and memories.

- **Application in Research:** Dr. Kapoor studies neuroplasticity to understand how the brain rewires itself in response to trauma or experiences. Fuzzy logic helps him simulate the varying degrees of neural connectivity, shedding light on how memory pathways may be strengthened or weakened, providing potential treatments for conditions like dementia or traumatic brain injuries.

d) Neurotransmitter

- **Definition:** Neurotransmitters are chemical messengers in the brain that transmit signals between neurons or from neurons to muscles. Key neurotransmitters include dopamine, serotonin, and acetylcholine, each of which influences various brain functions such as mood, motivation, and motor skills.

- **Dr. Kapoor's Use of Fuzzy Logic with Neurotransmitters:** Dr. Kapoor utilizes fuzzy logic to model the impact of neurotransmitter levels on neural activity, particularly in case of neurotransmitter imbalances like depression or Parkinson's disease. By simulating the graded effects of neurotransmitters, he explores therapies that might restore or modify neurochemical interactions.

e) Neurodegenerative Diseases

- **Definition:** Neurodegenerative diseases are a group of disorders characterized by progressive degeneration of neurons. Common neurodegenerative diseases include Alzheimer's disease, Parkinson's disease, and Huntington's disease.

- Fuzzy Logic in Studying Disease Progression: In his lab, Dr. Kapoor applies fuzzy logic to model the gradual onset and progression of neurodegenerative diseases. His research aims to create predictive models to identify early warning signs, which could improve interventions and slow down disease progression.

f) Neurophysiology

- Definition: Neurophysiology is the branch of neuroscience focused on the functions and activities of the nervous system, including how neurons communicate and how neural networks process information.

- Dr. Kapoor's Work as a Neurophysicist: Transitioning into neurophysiology allowed Dr. Kapoor to investigate how brain regions function and communicate on a cellular level. Fuzzy logic aids him in understanding the nuanced, continuous communication among neurons, which can vary in intensity and frequency, providing insights into how memory and cognition are physically encoded in the brain.

g) Neurological Disorders

- Definition: Neurological disorders encompass a wide range of conditions that affect the brain, spinal cord, and nerves, including epilepsy, multiple sclerosis, and migraines. These conditions can affect cognition, motor skills, sensation, and emotions.

- Research on Neurological Disorders: Dr. Kapoor's extensive work on neurological disorders includes studying seizure patterns in epilepsy and using fuzzy logic to model the probabilities of seizure onset. His goal is to identify patterns that traditional models overlook, helping predict and manage these disorders more effectively.

h) Neurochemical Interactions

- Definition: Neurochemical interactions refer to the complex exchanges between various neurotransmitters and receptors in the brain that regulate mood, behavior, and cognition.

- Application of Fuzzy Logic: In studying neurochemical interactions, Dr. Kapoor uses fuzzy logic to model subtle variations in neurotransmitter activity. This approach helps him better understand conditions like depression or addiction, where slight imbalances in neurochemical levels can have significant impacts on behavior and mental health.

i) Neurocomputational Models

- Definition: Neurocomputational models are simulations of brain processes that aim to replicate how neurons and neural networks operate. These models are often used in AI and machine learning applications that mimic human cognition.

- Use in Dr. Kapoor's Research: By employing fuzzy logic in neurocomputational models, Dr. Kapoor can create more flexible and realistic simulations of brain functions. This is particularly valuable for understanding complex cognitive functions like decision-making, where factors such as memory, emotions, and logic interact in non-linear ways.

j) Neurofeedback

• Definition: Neurofeedback is a technique that involves monitoring brain activity in real-time and providing feedback to help individuals learn to self-regulate brain functions. It's often used for treating conditions like ADHD, anxiety, and PTSD.

• Incorporation in Therapy: Dr. Kapoor is exploring neurofeedback as a potential treatment for memory disorders and cognitive decline. By using fuzzy logic, he aims to create adaptive Neurofeedback systems that respond to subtle shifts in brain activity, allowing patients to gradually regain control over certain cognitive functions.

k) Neurogenesis

• Definition: Neurogenesis is the process of generating new neurons in the brain, primarily occurring in regions such as the hippocampus, which is involved in memory formation and spatial navigation.

• Potential Research Area: Dr. Kapoor is interested in stimulating neurogenesis as a potential treatment for neurodegenerative diseases. Fuzzy logic could help identify the optimal conditions under which new neurons might form, offering a pathway for reversing some effects of brain aging and cognitive decline.

l) Neuroinformatics

- Definition: Neuroinformatics is a field at the intersection of neuroscience and information science, which involves organizing and analyzing large datasets from brain research.

- Fuzzy Logic in Data Analysis: In Dr. Kapoor's lab, neuroinformatics and fuzzy logic work hand-in-hand to process complex datasets from brain imaging and EEG studies. This combination allows his team to identify subtle patterns and variations in brain activity, which may offer new insights into cognitive function and neural disorders.

m) Neuropsychology

- Definition: Neuropsychology studies how brain function affects behavior and cognition, often focusing on the effects of brain injuries or neurological diseases.

- Dr. Kapoor's Interest in Neuropsychology: As Dr. Kapoor treats patients with memory loss and cognitive impairment, neuropsychology helps him understand the behavioral impact of brain dysfunctions. Fuzzy logic supports this by modeling the variability in individual responses to brain injuries, leading to more personalized and effective treatment plans.

n) Neuromodulation

- Definition: Neuromodulation is a technique that involves using electrical or chemical stimuli to regulate nerve activity in specific areas of the brain.

- Fuzzy Logic in Neuromodulation: Dr. Kapoor's research on Neuromodulation is enhanced by fuzzy logic, which helps tailor stimulation patterns for each patient. This personalized approach could improve treatments for patients with chronic pain, depression, or epilepsy by adjusting the stimulation levels based on the brain's fluctuating state.

o) Neurorehabilitation

- Definition: Neurorehabilitation involves therapies to improve the functioning of individuals who have suffered neurological damage, aiming to restore skills and quality of life.

- Use of Fuzzy Logic in Therapy Design: Dr. Kapoor integrates fuzzy logic into neurorehabilitation techniques, especially for patients with brain injuries. Fuzzy logic models allow therapists to adjust rehabilitation protocols based on the patient's ongoing recovery progress, creating a more adaptive and effective rehabilitation process.

The human brain is a marvel of evolution; three pounds of tissue capable of producing thoughts, emotions, and memories. Dr. Kapoor has dedicated his life to studying this miraculous organ, dissecting it layer by layer, cell by cell.

The brain is divided into various parts, each with distinct functions yet intricately connected. At the top lies the cerebrum, the largest part of the brain, divided into two hemispheres and responsible for complex thought processes. Its wrinkled surface, the cortex, houses billions of neurons involved in processing sensory data, emotions, and language.

Within the cerebrum, the frontal lobe is the seat of reasoning, problem-solving, and planning. This is where Dr. Kapoor focuses much of his research, especially in the study of memory. The parietal lobe integrates sensory information, allowing us to understand our surroundings. The temporal lobe is crucial for hearing and language, and contains the hippocampus, a seahorse-shaped structure integral to forming new memories. The occipital lobe, located at the back of the brain, processes visual information.

Underneath the cerebrum is the limbic system, which includes structures like the amygdala and hypothalamus, responsible for emotions and basic drives. The amygdala governs our instinctual responses, like fear and pleasure, while the hypothalamus regulates bodily functions such as hunger, thirst, and temperature.

Deeper still lies the brainstem, which connects the brain to the spinal cord. This primitive part of the brain controls survival functions breathing, heart rate, and sleep. The cerebellum, tucked underneath the occipital lobe, coordinates movement and balance.

3. **The Science of Memory: The Key to Dr. Kapoor's Success**

Memory is a complex and layered system within the brain, a process that enables humans to store and retrieve information. Dr. Kapoor, during his years of neurosurgical practice, developed an interest in memory systems, driven by the countless patients who had lost fragments of their identities to amnesia, Alzheimer's, and other conditions.

In his lab, Dr. Kapoor studies how neurons communicate to form and retain memories. Memory begins with encoding, a process by which sensory input is transformed into a form the brain can store. This data passes through the hippocampus and is consolidated into long-term memory in various regions of the neo-cortex. Dr. Kapoor often compares this process to a network of highways; each piece of information travels across multiple pathways until it finds a place to "settle" in the brain.

To better understand memory loss, Dr. Kapoor has spent years mapping the exact areas of the brain that retain different types of memories. His studies reveal that declarative memory which includes facts and events is primarily stored in the hippocampus and nearby structures. Meanwhile, procedural memory, responsible for skills and actions, is stored in the basal ganglia and cerebellum.

4. Diseases of the Brain: The Complexities and Challenges

One of Dr. Kapoor's goals is to uncover treatments for some of the most challenging brain disorders. His lab focuses on a range of conditions, from neurodegenerative diseases to brain injuries.

- Alzheimer's disease: Alzheimer's is marked by the buildup of plaques and tangles that slowly choke and kill neurons, leading to severe memory loss. Dr. Kapoor's research includes studying the proteins beta-amyloid and tau, which form these harmful structures. Through innovative imaging techniques, he works on identifying early indicators of Alzheimer's, aiming to treat the disease before significant neuronal damage occurs.

- Parkinson's disease: Parkinson's is a degenerative disorder affecting the dopamine-producing neurons in the substantia nigra. Dopamine is critical for controlling movement, and its depletion leads to tremors, stiffness, and difficulty with balance. Dr. Kapoor's work in deep brain stimulation (DBS) and advanced neuroimaging has led to promising treatments that mitigate symptoms, though he still seeks a cure.

- Epilepsy: Epilepsy results from abnormal electrical discharges in the brain, causing seizures. Dr. Kapoor uses EEG (electroencephalography) to study these irregular patterns and develop predictive models to warn patients of impending seizures.

- Traumatic Brain Injuries (TBIs): TBIs can have widespread effects, impacting memory, behavior, and cognitive function. Dr. Kapoor's team employs high-definition imaging to identify damaged areas and, in some cases, use stem cell therapy to regenerate neurons and restore lost functions.

- Mental Health Disorders: Dr. Kapoor is also invested in understanding the neurochemical imbalances underlying disorders like depression, schizophrenia, and PTSD. Through a combination of brain scans and neurotransmitter analysis, he examines the complex interplay of genetics, brain structure, and environmental triggers that give rise to these conditions.

5. The Paucity of Research in Neuroscience

Despite these advancements, Dr. Kapoor is acutely aware of the limitations of current neuroscience research. Funding is scarce, and the unpredictable nature of brain function often means that even the most promising treatments require years, if not decades, to develop.

The vast unknowns in brain research create a landscape where researchers struggle to secure funding without concrete, immediate results. Many brain regions, particularly those related to consciousness and perception, remain poorly understood. The challenges of accessing living human brain tissue, the ethical limitations of human testing, and the sheer complexity of the brain itself have all contributed to a lag in neurological studies.

Dr. Kapoor believes that greater international cooperation is needed. To advance his work, he advocates for a collaborative approach, envisioning a future where neuroscientists worldwide can share resources and findings through global databases, accelerating the pace of discovery.

6. Exploring Fuzzy Logic in Brain Research

A recent addition to Dr. Kapoor's toolkit is fuzzy logic, a mathematical system that allows for "degrees of truth" rather than simple binary distinctions. Fuzzy logic is particularly useful in understanding brain function, where most processes are not black and white but exist along a spectrum.

Using fuzzy logic, Dr. Kapoor builds algorithms that model the probability of neuron firing patterns in various cognitive states, such as fear, excitement, or stress. Instead of analyzing a neuron as "active" or "inactive," fuzzy systems can evaluate how active a neuron might be under specific conditions, offering more nuanced insights.

For example, fuzzy logic aids Dr. Kapoor in his study of decision-making. By simulating a scenario where the brain must weigh multiple choices, fuzzy logic can predict which networks of neurons are likely to engage based on past experiences stored in memory.

7. Towards the Future of Brain Research

Dr. Kapoor envisions a future where fuzzy logic, AI, and neuroscience merge seamlessly, creating tools that allow us not only to treat brain diseases but also to enhance brain function. His research suggests that with enough data, scientists may one day be able to predict and manipulate brain responses, leading to potential treatments for neurological disorders and perhaps even cognitive enhancement.

I hope this provides the level of depth you're looking for. We can continue expanding each section with specific examples, case studies, more technical descriptions of brain functions, and Dr. Kapoor's personal experiences with patients. Let me know if you'd like me to further develop a specific section or topic.

8. The Role of Fuzzy Logic in Decoding Brain Function

Fuzzy logic, a mathematical approach developed to handle degrees of uncertainty and ambiguity, has emerged as a powerful tool in Dr. Kapoor's research, especially as he ventures into the intricate and often unpredictable world of brain function. Unlike traditional binary logic, where outcomes are strictly "true" or "false," fuzzy logic allows for "degrees of truth," which better reflects the reality of biological processes. Dr. Kapoor believes that fuzzy logic provides a model more aligned with the brain's own fluid, nuanced operations.

In neuroscience, where signals and responses vary by intensity, time, and context, fuzzy logic has helped Dr. Kapoor and his team explores a range of phenomena:

Chapter Three - Neural Plasticity with Fuzzy Logic

1. Modeling Neural Plasticity with Fuzzy Logic

One of Dr. Kapoor's major interests is neural plasticity—the brain's ability to rewire itself in response to experiences, learning, or injuries. Traditional logic models struggle to accommodate the gradual, non-linear ways in which neurons and neural networks adapt. However, fuzzy logic allows Dr. Kapoor to simulate the changing levels of neuron connectivity more effectively.

By applying fuzzy sets, he can predict the likelihood of connections between neurons in various conditions, such as after trauma, during memory formation, or in response to medication. This approach helps him build models that reflect the true spectrum of neural adaptations, capturing "partial activations" within neurons, which may range from barely detectable signals to high-frequency firings. Dr. Kapoor uses these models to identify potential therapies for neurodegenerative diseases, allowing neurons to better adapt to or compensate for damaged areas.

2. Fuzzy Logic in Memory Retrieval and Formation

Memory formation and retrieval involve countless neurons, each with varying degrees of activation and interconnection. Dr. Kapoor found that fuzzy logic could effectively model these processes by accounting for degrees of similarity and partial matches in memory recall.

For example, when a person tries to recall a familiar face but can't quite place it, certain neurons are partially activated. These activations do not fully reach the threshold for a complete memory recall but suggest a "fuzzy" familiarity. Dr. Kapoor uses fuzzy algorithms to map this partial activation and identify the specific neurons involved in such fuzzy memories. This research has implications for treating memory disorders, as it may allow targeted stimulation of neurons to "strengthen" fuzzy memories or reinforce partially lost connections in patients with Alzheimer's disease.

3. Decision-Making and Emotional Responses

Decision-making in the human brain is rarely straightforward. It is influenced by a complex mix of emotions, past experiences, and subconscious drives. Dr. Kapoor has applied fuzzy logic to better understand how the brain processes these factors simultaneously.

For instance, fuzzy logic allows Dr. Kapoor to model how the amygdala, which processes emotions, interacts with the prefrontal cortex, where rational decisions are formed. Emotions like fear, anticipation, and doubt often coexist, influencing decisions to varying degrees. Dr. Kapoor's models using fuzzy logic can simulate how different emotional weights influence the brain's decision-making process. This has practical applications for developing therapeutic techniques to help individuals with conditions like anxiety and PTSD manage overwhelming emotions by regulating their cognitive-emotional balance.

4. Predicting Seizure Patterns with Fuzzy Logic

Epileptic seizures arise from abnormal bursts of neuronal activity, yet their onset is notoriously difficult to predict. Fuzzy logic provides a way to create predictive models for seizure activity by identifying small variations in electrical signals, which might indicate an upcoming seizure but do not necessarily reach the threshold of detection by traditional methods.

Dr. Kapoor's lab uses fuzzy algorithms to analyze EEG data, detecting subtle, gradual shifts in neural activity that could signal a high likelihood of a seizure. Fuzzy logic's capacity to interpret partial, ambiguous signals enables earlier detection and possibly preemptive intervention, improving the quality of life for individuals with epilepsy.

5. Manipulating Neurochemical Interactions

The brain's functions rely on complex interactions between neurons and neurotransmitters, which are chemicals like dopamine, serotonin, and acetylcholine. Each neurotransmitter operates differently depending on concentrations, neuron receptors, and timing. Dr. Kapoor employs fuzzy logic to model these neurochemical interactions, focusing on neurotransmitters' graded effects rather than viewing them as simple on-off switches.

For instance, dopamine plays a key role in reward, pleasure, and motor function and its levels can vary widely in different regions of the brain. By creating fuzzy models of dopamine's variable effects, Dr. Kapoor's team can analyze how different concentrations influence emotions and behavior, from joy and motivation to addiction and compulsion. This research offers insights into therapies for disorders like Parkinson's disease, depression, and addiction, where neurotransmitter levels are often imbalanced.

6. Developing Fuzzy Logic Systems for Brain-Computer Interfaces

Brain-computer interfaces (BCIs) are devices that allow direct communication between the brain and external devices, such as computers or prosthetics. Dr. Kapoor is pioneering research on BCIs using fuzzy logic, which can interpret the brain's intentions more flexibly by analyzing electrical signals with varying degrees of intensity.

With fuzzy logic, BCIs can distinguish between subtle changes in mental states, making devices more responsive and adaptable. For instance, a BCI equipped with fuzzy algorithms might better interpret slight variations in a patient's focus, excitement, or fatigue, allowing smoother interactions. This is particularly helpful for patients with neurodegenerative diseases or severe paralysis, where fine-tuning the brain's commands to control a prosthetic arm or cursor on a screen can greatly enhance their quality of life.

7. Probabilistic Models for Neurodegenerative Disease Progression

Dr. Kapoor also uses fuzzy logic to model the progression of neurodegenerative diseases, like Alzheimer's and Parkinson's, where symptoms manifest gradually. Fuzzy logic allows him to create probabilistic models that capture early, subtle signs of degeneration, identifying patterns that might otherwise be overlooked.

By assessing "degrees" of cognitive impairment—such as minor memory lapses or slight coordination issues—Dr. Kapoor's fuzzy-based models can forecast how quickly a disease might progress and tailor treatment plans accordingly. These models offer a more individualized approach to patient care, with predictions on when a patient might need more intensive therapy or monitoring.

8. Future Applications of Fuzzy Logic in Dr. Kapoor's Research

Dr. Kapoor's use of fuzzy logic is opening doors to advanced areas of brain research that are still largely unexplored. He envisions a future where fuzzy logic could be applied to simulate and perhaps even "enhance" cognitive functions. For example, fuzzy systems might allow the controlled strengthening of particular neural networks, improving areas like learning, memory, or emotional resilience.

Moreover, with advances in machine learning and AI, Dr. Kapoor plans to merge fuzzy logic with these technologies to create adaptive neural models capable of predicting brain responses in real time. This could potentially transform treatments for a variety of conditions, from mood disorders to traumatic brain injuries.

This detailed exploration of fuzzy logic in Dr. Kapoor's work captures the potential of this mathematical approach in neuroscience, reflecting its profound implications for understanding and treating complex brain functions. Let me know if you'd like to expand further on any specific aspect, or if you need additional areas covered.

Chapter Four - The Science of Memory and Neural Connections

This chapter takes an in-depth journey into memory – the brain's extraordinary ability to record, store, and retrieve information. Memory shapes identity, informs decision-making, and is integral to how we interpret and respond to the world. Neuroscientists continue to uncover the complexities of memory, yet much remains unknown. In this chapter, we will investigate how neurons create and maintain memory, what happens when memory deteriorates, and potential avenues for memory preservation and retrieval.

1. Introduction to Memory: The Brain's Data Archive

Memory is essentially the brain's way of encoding, storing, and accessing information. Memories can range from something as transient as a fleeting impression of a smell to a deeply ingrained fact or skill. Neurons and synaptic connections are essential to memory creation and retrieval. As neurons interact and establish connections, they form intricate networks that represent specific pieces of information. Each time we recall a memory, these connections are reactivated, strengthening the associations.

Memory Storage Locations: The human brain contains several regions responsible for different aspects of memory. Key areas include:

❖ Hippocampus: Central to forming new memories, especially episodic (event-based) memories.

❖ Amygdala: Plays a role in emotional memories, connecting emotions with certain events.

❖ Cortex: Involved in long-term memory storage and is believed to handle semantic (fact-based) memories.

❖ Cerebellum: Crucial for procedural memories, such as motor skills.

2. Types of Memory and Their Characteristics

Memory is categorized based on how long information is retained and the kind of information it processes. Each type of memory involves different brain regions and pathways, often working together to create a cohesive memory experience.

❖ Sensory Memory: The briefest type of memory, capturing impressions from the five senses for just milliseconds. It quickly fades unless attention is focused on it.

❖ Short-Term (Working) Memory: This form of memory holds small amounts of information for seconds to minutes, such as remembering a phone number before dialing it. It involves the prefrontal cortex and is critical for tasks requiring immediate use of information.

❖ Long-Term Memory: Long-term memory is stored for days, years, or even a lifetime. It has two main types:

o Explicit (Declarative) Memory: Memories that require conscious recall, including:

- Semantic Memory: Facts and general knowledge.
- Episodic Memory: Personal experiences or events.

o Implicit (Procedural) Memory: Skills and actions that become automatic, such as typing or riding a bicycle. Stored in the basal ganglia and cerebellum, these memories do not require conscious recall.

From Short-Term to Long-Term Storage: The process of converting short-term memory into long-term storage, known as memory consolidation, primarily occurs in the hippocampus. Once consolidated, memories are distributed across the cortex for more permanent storage.

3. Memory Disorders and Their Impact on Neurons

Numerous memory disorders arise due to damage, disease, or degeneration of neurons. These disorders vary widely, affecting everything from memory formation to recall.

❖ Alzheimer's disease: A degenerative disease characterized by plaques and tangles in the brain, disrupting neuron function and leading to progressive memory loss and cognitive decline. Alzheimer's involves significant loss of neurons in the hippocampus and cortex.

❖ Dementia: A general term describing symptoms that include memory loss, reasoning impairment, and disorientation. Dementia may result from multiple causes, including vascular damage, Lewy body disease, and brain injury.

❖ Amnesia: Memory impairment caused by damage to memory-related brain structures. Amnesia can be:

o Retrograde Amnesia: Loss of pre-existing memories.

o Anterograde Amnesia: Inability to form new memories, often resulting from hippocampus damage.

❖ Age-Related Memory Decline: The aging process naturally reduces neuron health and decreases synaptic plasticity, impacting memory retrieval and cognitive speed. While this is a normal process, it may contribute to mild forgetfulness.

4. Neuron Damage, Signal Loss, and Memory Erosion

Neurons are the fundamental units for memory storage and retrieval, and their deterioration directly affects memory capability.

❖ Neuron Erosion: Neurons can deteriorate from disease, injury, or age. When neurons in the hippocampus or cortex die, memory loss occurs as the neural networks representing these memories break down.

❖ Synaptic Damage: Memories are encoded in the connections (synapses) between neurons. If these synapses are damaged, either through neurodegenerative disease or trauma, it disrupts memory circuits and can lead to memory deficits.

❖ Signal Capability Loss: Neurons communicate through electrical and chemical signals. When neurons are damaged, the signals weaken or stop, leading to memory impairment as connections deteriorate.

Reversing Neuron Damage: Research into neurogenesis, or neuron regeneration, shows promise, especially in areas like the hippocampus. Stem cell therapy, neurotrophic drugs, and synapse-strengthening agents may help repair neuron damage and restore limited memory function in early stages of disorders.

5. Innovations in Memory Preservation and External Storage

Given the challenges of neuron loss and aging, scientists are exploring ways to preserve and store memories outside the human brain.

❖ Digital Storage of Memory: The concept of "memory uploading" would involve mapping synaptic connections to digitally store memories. This remains theoretical, but advances in neuroscience and computing are pushing the boundaries.

❖ Creating Neurofunctional Devices: Future devices could potentially replicate brain structures to store information from neural patterns, allowing a person's memories to be accessed after they pass or become impaired.

❖ Challenges in Digital Memory: Transferring memories is not only technically complex but ethically fraught, involving questions of identity, privacy, and the nature of consciousness.

6. Memory Transplantation and Restoration Possibilities

As neuroscience advances, new questions emerge about the potential for transplanting or restoring memories in cases of extreme memory loss.

❖ Memory Restoration: If memory storage can be understood down to neural patterns, scientists may be able to restore lost memories by re-establishing those patterns artificially.

❖ Memory Implantation in Alternative Brains: With enough understanding of neural encoding, it may be feasible to implant memories into another brain. This could involve transferring memories from someone who passed away to a recipient with cognitive impairments or "blank slate" areas in their brain.

❖ Applications for Critical Situations: For individuals facing life-threatening conditions, the ability to save their memories externally may allow future restoration if they recover or if another recipient is identified.

7. Fuzzy Logic and Neuroengineering in Memory Research

Fuzzy logic is an approach that allows for more flexible, nuanced computations than binary logic, which is particularly suited to brain research where absolute "yes" or "no" outcomes are rare.

❖ Mapping Complex Neural Processes: Memory and neuron interactions are not strictly linear. Fuzzy logic allows neuroscientists to model the brain's associative patterns more accurately, capturing the "gray areas" in neuron behavior and signal processing.

❖ Adaptive Memory Devices: In neuroengineering, fuzzy logic could support the creation of adaptive devices that interpret partial or varied neural signals, mimicking how the brain stores and recalls memories based on context.

❖ Memory Recovery and Fuzzy Logic: For patients with memory impairments, fuzzy logic can potentially aid in creating adaptive therapies, interpreting neural signals during recall attempts to make memory retrieval more effective and individualized.

Chapter Two, Three and Four illuminate the profound complexities of memory and the neuron-based networks that make memory possible. Through exploring memory types, disorders, neuron health, and potential innovations in memory preservation, we see how intricate and fragile the memory process is. With ongoing research in fuzzy logic and neuroengineering, the future may hold answers to previously unimaginable questions, like memory restoration and even memory transplantation. This chapter offers a foundation for understanding the promise and ethical considerations in our pursuit to unravel the mysteries of memory in the human brain.

Chapter Five - The Science of Hypnotism – A Neuroscientific Approach

Hypnotism, often surrounded by mystique, is a psychological state that can significantly influence a person's perceptions, memories, and behaviors. While it's frequently misrepresented in popular culture, hypnotism is a well-documented phenomenon with practical applications in various fields, including medicine and psychotherapy. This chapter delves into the definitions, mechanisms, types, and clinical applications of hypnosis, particularly how it interacts with the brain and influences behavior.

1. Definitions and Key Terminologies in Hypnotism

To understand hypnotism, it's essential to familiarize ourselves with foundational terminology:

❖ Hypnotism: The art and science of inducing a state of altered consciousness in which an individual experiences heightened focus and suggestibility. Hypnotism can create profound psychological and physiological effects, depending on the depth of the trance and the intent of the hypnotist.

- ❖ Hypnosis: The state of focused attention and reduced peripheral awareness in which a person may be more responsive to suggestions. Hypnosis involves entering a trance-like condition where conscious control over behavior is partially or fully bypassed.

- ❖ Trance: A state of deep relaxation, intense focus, and selective attention. During trance, external distractions are minimized, allowing for a greater influence of the hypnotist's suggestions.

- ❖ Suggestibility: The degree to which a person is receptive to suggestions or commands given by another, often heightened in a state of hypnosis. This phenomenon is the key to understanding why hypnotized individuals might perform or recall things they wouldn't ordinarily.

- ❖ Post-Hypnotic Suggestion: A suggestion made during hypnosis that the person follows after coming out of the trance. This is useful for therapeutic purposes, such as reducing anxiety or breaking unwanted habits.

- ❖ Hypnotherapy: The use of hypnosis as a therapeutic tool to treat psychological and physiological conditions. Licensed hypnotherapists employ various techniques to help patients overcome issues like chronic pain, addiction, and trauma.

2. Types of Hypnosis

Hypnosis can be categorized based on the method of induction, purpose, and level of control exerted over the individual. Here are some common types:

❖ Traditional (Direct) Hypnosis: Involves direct suggestions to the subconscious, often used for therapeutic purposes. It's straightforward and usually involves a hypnotist guiding the subject into a trance and offering direct commands or suggestions.

❖ Ericksonian (Indirect) Hypnosis: Named after Dr. Milton Erickson, this approach uses metaphorical and indirect suggestions rather than commands. It's more conversational and engages the subject's imagination and subconscious in a subtle way.

❖ Self-Hypnosis: A self-induced hypnotic state, often used to manage stress, reduce anxiety, or prepare for a performance. The individual practices techniques to enter a state of focused relaxation without a hypnotherapist's guidance.

❖ Stage Hypnosis: Primarily used for entertainment, this involves hypnotizing willing participants to perform unusual or amusing actions. This form, while less scientific, relies on the subject's suggestibility and willingness to engage in entertaining activities.

❖ Guided Hypnosis (Guided Imagery): Often used in therapy, guided hypnosis involves verbal instructions to help the subject visualize calming scenes. It's beneficial for relaxation, stress relief, and even pain management.

❖ Cognitive Behavioral Hypnosis (CBH): This form integrates cognitive behavioral techniques with hypnosis, focusing on changing thought patterns and behaviors. It is commonly used in clinical therapy to treat anxiety and addiction.

3. Uses of Hypnosis

Hypnosis has broad applications, particularly in medicine and psychology:

❖ Pain Management: Hypnosis can help patients manage chronic pain by influencing how the brain perceives pain signals. It's especially useful for those suffering from arthritis, migraines, or post-surgical discomfort.

❖ Anxiety and Depression Treatment: Hypnotherapy allows patients to explore their emotions in a safe environment, encouraging them to confront and process deep-seated anxieties or depressive thoughts.

❖ Phobias and Habit Control: Hypnosis is effective in treating phobias by desensitizing the individual to their fears. It's also used to address habits like smoking, nail-biting, and overeating by making the subject more receptive to healthier behavioral alternatives.

❖ Stress Reduction and Relaxation: Hypnosis promotes deep relaxation and is widely used for stress management. Many people practice self-hypnosis or guided imagery to relax after a stressful day.

❖ Surgical Preparation and Recovery: Hypnosis helps patients prepare mentally for surgery, reducing anxiety. It's also shown to expedite recovery by helping patients remain calm and positive post-surgery.

4. Misuse of Hypnosis

While hypnosis has numerous beneficial applications, it can also be misused in certain situations:

❖ Memory Manipulation: Hypnosis can influence the recall process, leading to "false memories." This can be problematic, especially in legal contexts where memories retrieved under hypnosis may be inaccurate or fabricated.

❖ Coercive Hypnosis: Hypnosis may make subjects more suggestible, and unscrupulous individuals can exploit this to make them act against their best interests. However, it is generally accepted that people cannot be made to do anything deeply against their values, even under hypnosis.

❖ Dependency Issues: Over-reliance on hypnosis as a coping mechanism can result in dependency, where individuals may avoid addressing problems directly and rely on hypnosis for every issue.

5. Hypnosis in Neurosurgery and Neuroscience

Hypnosis offers unique advantages in neurosurgery and other medical practices:

❖ Hypnotic Anesthesia: For patients who cannot tolerate anesthesia, hypnosis can help reduce pain and anxiety during surgery. Surgeons can use hypnotic techniques to induce a calm state, minimizing discomfort and stabilizing vital signs.

❖ Cognitive Recovery and Rehabilitation: Neurosurgeons use hypnosis to aid recovery in patients who have suffered from strokes or traumatic brain injuries. By reinforcing positive mental images and encouraging motor skill recall, hypnosis can accelerate rehabilitation.

❖ Pain Control in Postoperative Care: After brain or spinal surgery, hypnosis helps control pain, potentially reducing the need for heavy painkillers, which can have adverse effects. It also promotes faster recovery by encouraging relaxation.

6. Neuroscientific Mechanisms of Hypnosis: What Happens in the Brain?

During hypnosis, several specific brain regions are activated, and neurotransmitter levels shift, resulting in an altered state of consciousness:

❖ The Prefrontal Cortex: This area, associated with decision-making and attention, shows reduced activity during hypnosis, enabling a state of mental relaxation and focus.

❖ The Anterior Cingulate Cortex (ACC): Responsible for attention control and error detection, the ACC becomes highly active during hypnosis. It allows individuals to focus intensely on suggestions while blocking out distractions.

❖ Thalamus: This "relay station" for sensory signals also alters its activity in a hypnotic state. Hypnosis seems to reduce thalamic activity, which filters out extraneous sensory information, thereby enhancing focus on hypnotic suggestions.

❖ Default Mode Network (DMN): This network, active when the mind is at rest and reflective, becomes less active during hypnosis, leading to a state of immersion. Reduced DMN activity is associated with decreased self-awareness and a higher susceptibility to suggestion.

❖ Neurotransmitter Changes: Hypnosis influences dopamine and endorphin release, which play roles in motivation, focus, and pain relief, contributing to the sense of relaxation and reduced discomfort during hypnosis.

7. Why Hypnotized Individuals Respond to Suggestions

The brain's altered state during hypnosis makes individuals more receptive to suggestions for several reasons:

❖ Selective Attention: The narrowing of focus during hypnosis is so intense that individuals tune out competing thoughts and environmental stimuli, concentrating entirely on the hypnotist's words.

❖ Reduced Critical Judgment: Due to decreased activity in the prefrontal cortex, hypnotized individuals may suspend their usual judgment and skepticism, making them more willing to accept commands.

❖ State of Hyper-Suggestibility: Hypnosis creates a unique mental state where the boundary between conscious and subconscious thinking is thin, leading to enhanced suggestibility. This allows the hypnotist's instructions to be accepted more readily and acted upon without internal resistance.

8. The Future of Hypnosis: Brain-Computer Interfaces and Neurofeedback

Neuroscientists are exploring innovative ways to combine hypnosis with advanced technologies, such as:

❖ Brain-Computer Interfaces (BCIs): BCIs could allow for more precise inductions of hypnotic states by monitoring brain waves and providing real-time feedback. For example, EEG feedback could enable a hypnotist to guide a subject into an optimal hypnotic state.

❖ Neurofeedback and Customized Hypnosis: Neurofeedback training helps individuals enter a self-hypnotic state by guiding them to achieve specific brain wave patterns. This personalized approach may improve the effectiveness of therapeutic hypnosis.

Observation

Hypnosis is a scientifically validated phenomenon with complex mechanisms rooted in neurobiology. While often misunderstood, its applications extend far beyond entertainment. Neurosurgeons, psychologists, and pain management specialists are increasingly incorporating hypnosis to improve outcomes and support patients in ways conventional medicine may not. With new insights from neuroscience and emerging technologies, hypnosis holds even greater potential as an invaluable tool in both medical and therapeutic settings.

Chapter Six - Concept of Neuroengineering

Neuroengineering

Neuroengineering is a highly interdisciplinary field combining principles from neuroscience, engineering, computer science, and biology to develop technologies and methods that interact with the nervous system, particularly the brain. It aims to understand, repair, enhance, and even emulate neurological function, creating solutions that can treat or compensate for a variety of neurological conditions and injuries. Here's a closer look at its fundamental concepts, applications, and future potential:

a) What is Neuroengineering?

Neuroengineering, also known as neural engineering, applies engineering techniques to the nervous system. It involves the design and application of tools to understand how the brain functions, how to measure and manipulate neural activity, and how to replace lost functions when areas of the brain are damaged. This field integrates neuroscience's deep understanding of the brain with engineering's focus on problem-solving, often through innovative hardware, algorithms, and biofeedback systems.

b) Core Components of Neuroengineering

✓ Brain-Machine Interfaces (BMIs): These are systems that allow direct communication between the brain and external devices, such as computers or prosthetics. BMIs are commonly used in neuroprosthetics, where they enable patients with limb loss or paralysis to control artificial limbs or assistive devices using only their thoughts.

✓ Neuroprosthetics: Neuroprosthetics involve devices that restore lost sensory or motor functions by electrically stimulating the nervous system. Examples include cochlear implants for hearing loss, retinal implants for vision impairment, and spinal cord stimulators for chronic pain relief. Neuroprosthetics can also be used for deep brain stimulation in conditions like Parkinson's disease, where precise electrical impulses can alleviate tremors and other symptoms.

✓ Neural Implants: Devices implanted in the brain can monitor or stimulate neural activity. For example, electrode arrays can be implanted in specific brain areas to treat movement disorders, monitor seizure activity in epilepsy, or research how neurons communicate. Implants can also be part of BMIs or used in experimental treatments for mental health disorders.

✓ Signal Processing and Neural Decoding: Neuroengineers develop algorithms to analyze complex brain signals, making sense of the data collected from neural activity. This process, known as neural decoding, is essential for BMIs, as it translates the brain's electrical signals into commands for devices, allowing for real-time interaction.

✓ Optogenetics and Neuromodulation: Optogenetics is a technique where neurons are genetically modified to respond to light, enabling precise control of neural activity. Neuromodulation, more broadly, includes methods like transcranial magnetic stimulation (TMS) and transcranial direct current stimulation (tDCS), which non-invasively stimulate specific brain regions to treat depression, anxiety, or chronic pain.

c) Applications of Neuroengineering

Neuroengineering has the potential to impact several areas of healthcare and beyond:

✓ Treatment of Neurological Disorders: Neuroengineering provides innovative treatments for epilepsy, Alzheimer's disease, Parkinson's disease, and more. By understanding and influencing brain signals, neuroengineers develop therapies that can alleviate symptoms or even halt disease progression.

✓ Restoration of Movement and Sensation: Neuroprosthetics and BMIs are helping patients with spinal cord injuries, amputations, or neurological conditions regain some movement or sensation. Patients can learn to control robotic limbs, powered wheelchairs, or computer cursors, improving their quality of life significantly.

✓ Mental Health Interventions: Neuroengineering techniques like deep brain stimulation and TMS are being used to treat severe depression, obsessive-compulsive disorder (OCD), and other mental health conditions. These treatments target specific brain areas to alter neural circuits related to mood and behavior, offering hope to those who have not responded to traditional therapies.

✓ Cognitive Enhancement and Memory Restoration: Research in neuroengineering is exploring ways to enhance memory or reverse memory loss. Experimental devices, often called "memory prosthetics," aim to stimulate hippocampal neurons to mimic natural memory processes. These devices have potential applications in Alzheimer's treatment and cognitive enhancement.

✓ Brain-Computer Interactions for Learning and Communication: For individuals with communication impairments due to conditions like ALS or stroke, neuroengineering can create interfaces that allow them to express thoughts directly through a computer. Such systems rely on decoding thought patterns or motor intentions from neural activity, translating them into text or speech.

d) Challenges in Neuroengineering

While the field holds immense promise, neuroengineering also faces numerous challenges:

✓ Precision and Complexity: The human brain is incredibly complex, with billions of neurons and trillions of synapses. Mapping and influencing brain activity with precision requires advances in both technology and our understanding of neural circuits.

✓ Ethical and Privacy Concerns: Neuroengineering raises ethical questions, especially regarding BMIs and memory manipulation. There are concerns about privacy, autonomy, and the potential for misuse, as brain signals could reveal sensitive information or lead to unauthorized control over neural processes.

✓ Longevity and Biocompatibility: Implants and devices used in the brain must be biocompatible to avoid immune rejection or degradation. They must also maintain functionality over time to be practical for long-term treatment.

✓ Data Processing and Interpretation: Brain signals are noisy, complex, and vary between individuals. Developing accurate, adaptive algorithms that interpret neural data consistently remains a substantial technical challenge.

e)   Future Directions in Neuroengineering

The future of neuroengineering is evolving toward even more personalized, efficient, and non-invasive interventions. Areas of active research include:

✓ Closed-Loop Systems: These systems allow real-time feedback between the brain and devices. For example, a closed-loop BMI could adjust stimulation based on changes in brain activity, enhancing precision and reducing side effects in applications like neuroprosthetics.

✓ Memory Prosthetics: Building devices that can mimic the encoding, storage, and recall of memories is a current focus in neuroengineering. Early-stage research involves stimulating the hippocampus to recreate the electrical patterns involved in memory formation, which may one day help restore lost memories in patients with Alzheimer's or traumatic brain injuries.

✓ Advanced Neuromodulation Techniques: New methods of brain stimulation, such as ultrasound-based stimulation, could allow for more targeted and non-invasive interventions. Such techniques may be more comfortable and safer for patients than traditional invasive methods.

✓ Artificial Intelligence in Neural Decoding: AI can significantly enhance the decoding of complex brain signals by recognizing patterns that humans might miss. Machine learning algorithms are being developed to improve BMIs, making them more responsive and intuitive to use.

f) Observation

Neuroengineering is pushing the boundaries of what we can achieve in understanding, treating, and enhancing the brain's capabilities. By bridging neuroscience and engineering, it holds the potential to transform the treatment of neurological and psychiatric disorders, improve quality of life for individuals with impairments, and even augment human abilities. However, with this progress comes a need for ethical consideration, as the manipulation and monitoring of brain activity raise new challenges regarding autonomy, privacy, and the nature of human consciousness itself.

Mass Hypnosis is the phenomenon of influencing or putting a large group of people into a suggestible state where they can be led to think, feel, or behave in particular ways. It is often linked to large-scale persuasion techniques used by charismatic leaders, media, advertising, or political figures. Though it does not resemble the one-on-one hypnosis used in therapy, it draws on similar principles of suggestion, repetition, and psychological influence to guide people toward certain beliefs or actions. Below is an in-depth look at how mass hypnosis works, its mechanisms, and its potential benefits and drawbacks.

g) How Mass Hypnosis Works

Mass hypnosis relies on several psychological and environmental factors to place groups of people in a heightened state of suggestibility. While traditional hypnosis typically involves relaxation and focused attention in a quiet environment, mass hypnosis operates in larger, often more dynamic settings, but still taps into similar mechanisms:

➢ The Power of Suggestion: In mass hypnosis, suggestions are repeated and reinforced. Leaders, speakers, or media deliver specific messages in a confident, often repetitive manner to instill ideas. Repeated statements, especially when delivered with authority, can create a sense of familiarity and credibility, leading people to accept them as truth.

➢ Group Dynamics and Social Influence: People are highly influenced by those around them. In group settings, individuals tend to conform to the behavior and beliefs of others, especially when others appear to be in agreement. This herd mentality can make people more receptive to suggestions, particularly if others in the group seem convinced.

➢ Emotional Triggers: Mass hypnosis often leverages emotions such as fear, hope, or excitement to heighten suggestibility. Emotional arousal, such as through stirring speeches, music, or visuals, can bypass rational thinking and lead people to accept ideas without critical examination. For example, political rallies or advertising campaigns often use powerful imagery and messages to evoke emotions, creating a receptive mental state.

➢ Authority and Credibility: People are more likely to accept ideas or instructions from those they perceive as experts or figures of authority. When a leader speaks with confidence and assurance, their perceived authority can make audiences more willing to follow and believe in their words.

➢ Altered Consciousness and Attention Control: Mass hypnosis doesn't put people into a deep trance like traditional hypnosis, but it does create a light trance-like state by capturing and controlling attention. Repeated exposure to certain ideas, slogans, or imagery can shift people's consciousness to a more focused, less critical state, making them more open to suggestion.

➢ Repetition and Consistency: The more often a message is repeated, the more familiar and acceptable it becomes to people. This "mere exposure effect" can make even questionable ideas seem normal or reasonable over time, leading people to adopt them without deeper analysis.

h) Examples of Mass Hypnosis in Action

➢ Political Rallies and Campaigns: Leaders often use emotionally charged language, repetition of slogans, and displays of national symbols to create a shared identity and influence the collective mind. Speeches, chants, and crowd dynamics create an atmosphere where individuals feel connected to a larger cause and are open to adopting the views presented.

➢ Media and Advertising: Brands and advertisers use visual and audio repetition, emotional storytelling, and authority figures (like celebrities) to shape public opinion and behavior. For example, ads that repeatedly portray certain products as essential to happiness or success can influence people's purchasing decisions.

➢ Religious Gatherings: In some religious ceremonies, chants, music, and repetitive rituals can lead groups into a state of collective focus or euphoria.

This environment can heighten suggestibility and make people more receptive to the ideas presented.

i) Pros of Mass Hypnosis

➢ Promotes Unity and Shared Goals: Mass hypnosis can bring people together for a common cause, creating a sense of unity. It can be used positively in social movements, charity drives, and community building, motivating people to work together toward a collective goal.

➢ Inspiration and Motivation: Charismatic leaders often use mass hypnosis techniques to inspire and energize people, helping them find courage or motivation to pursue positive changes. In business, this can lead to higher morale and productivity, while in social causes, it can encourage positive action.

➢ Therapeutic Potential in Group Settings: In a controlled environment, some forms of mass hypnosis can be used in group therapy settings to address shared issues like stress, anxiety, or addiction. Techniques used in these settings are generally more supportive, focusing on encouraging healthier behaviors.

j) Cons of Mass Hypnosis

➢ Manipulation and Loss of Autonomy: Mass hypnosis can be misused to manipulate people's thoughts and behaviors without their informed consent. Political leaders, cult leaders, or media figures can exploit people's suggestibility, leading them to adopt beliefs or perform actions that may not align with their personal values.

➤ Reduced Critical Thinking: Mass hypnosis often bypasses critical analysis, leading people to accept information without questioning its accuracy. This can result in the spread of misinformation or harmful ideologies, as people fail to assess the validity of what they're hearing.

➤ Risk of Harmful Behaviors: In extreme cases, people under the influence of mass hypnosis may engage in harmful or dangerous behaviors that they might not normally consider. Cults or extremist groups sometimes use mass hypnotic techniques to coerce followers into acts they would otherwise avoid.

➤ Emotional and Psychological Impact: Constant exposure to emotionally charged suggestions can lead to chronic stress, anxiety, or feelings of disillusionment, especially if the message involves fear or manipulation. Individuals may develop a heightened sense of dependence on authority figures or a belief system that restricts their personal growth.

k) Neurological Mechanisms of Mass Hypnosis

During mass hypnosis, certain parts of the brain are more active or receptive to suggestion. These include:

➤ Amygdala: The amygdala is involved in processing emotions, particularly fear and excitement. Emotional arousal activates the amygdala, creating a heightened sense of alertness that makes people more receptive to suggestions.

➢ Prefrontal Cortex: The prefrontal cortex is responsible for decision-making and critical thinking. Mass hypnosis can create a temporary "override" effect, where emotional arousal reduces prefrontal cortex activity, leading people to accept suggestions without careful consideration.

➢ Mirror Neurons: Mirror neurons play a role in empathy and imitation, allowing us to mirror the emotions and actions of those around us. In group settings, these neurons may cause individuals to adopt the behaviors, emotions, or beliefs of others in the crowd, reinforcing conformity and groupthink.

➢ Anterior Cingulate Cortex: This region of the brain helps control attention and focus. Mass hypnosis often involves sustained attention on a speaker or message, activating this area and facilitating a trance-like focus where people become more open to suggestion.

l)   Ethical Considerations of Mass Hypnosis

While mass hypnosis can be used for positive purposes, it raises ethical questions:

➢ Informed Consent: People may not realize they are being influenced, which raises issues about consent. Ethically, individuals should be aware of and agree to participate in any process that could alter their thoughts or behaviors.

➢ Responsibility of Influence: Leaders or speakers who use mass hypnosis hold significant power, making it essential that they act responsibly and prioritize the well-being of their audience.

➤ Potential for Coercion: Using mass hypnosis to coerce individuals into behaviors that go against their values or interests is highly unethical and can lead to psychological harm.

m) Observation

Mass hypnosis is a powerful tool that can inspire and unify but also manipulate and harm. Its effectiveness relies on the natural suggestibility of humans in group settings, especially when emotional arousal and authority come into play. When used ethically, it can foster positive changes and inspire collective action; however, when misused, it has the potential to reduce critical thinking, promote harmful ideologies, and undermine individual autonomy. Understanding the psychological and neurological mechanisms of mass hypnosis can help people recognize when it's being used and develop strategies to maintain autonomy and critical thinking in high-pressure group settings.

Chapter Seven - Somesh the Healer

1. The Awakening in the Hills

Dr. Aryan Kapoor's book, Mysteries of Our Brain, was a sensation from the moment it hit the shelves. The scientific world applauded it, families found it enlightening, and individuals all across the country eagerly grabbed copies, intrigued by Dr. Kapoor's deep dive into the intricacies of human memory, consciousness, and the brain's untapped mysteries. But not everyone who picked up this groundbreaking work had noble intentions. As with any powerful knowledge, Dr. Kapoor's discoveries had the potential for both great good and profound harm.

Nestled in the rugged hills of India's northeastern border, on the fringes of the India-Myanmar boundary, was a small, hidden village. Its inhabitants led a quiet life, their days shaped by the cycles of nature and the traditions passed down from their ancestors. The village had remained relatively untouched by the modern world. Its rustic charm lay in its simplicity—a collection of wooden and stone houses scattered along winding paths, embraced by dense forests and rugged cliffs that seemed to merge into the clouds. Life here moved at a pace different from the rest of the world. Villagers rose with the sun and tended to their livestock or worked in the fields, while the children played in the narrow, cobbled streets.

In one of the village's small, dilapidated huts, a man named Somesh sat reading Dr. Kapoor's book intently. Somesh was in his early forties, with a weathered face and piercing eyes that betrayed a mind far sharper than his modest surroundings suggested. As a self-taught healer and practitioner of hypnosis, Somesh had devoted his life to the service of the villagers. Through hypnotic techniques and natural remedies, he helped ease their pains, cure ailments, and, occasionally, alleviate deeply buried traumas. Though he had never sought or expected financial reward, his services earned him immense respect among the villagers.

For the past two days, Somesh had been consumed by Dr. Kapoor's book. He read it from cover to cover multiple times, deeply focused on every paragraph, every word, particularly in the chapters that discussed memory and hypnosis. For Somesh, this was more than just a book—it was a revelation, a treasure trove of knowledge about the human brain that he hadn't previously grasped. Dr. Kapoor's explanations on memory locations and the brain's capability for hypnotic influence fascinated him beyond measure. Here was science finally describing the very arts he had practiced all his life.

As he continued to read, a thought stirred within him—an idea that, once it took hold, refused to let go. For years, he had lived humbly, helping people as best he could, but never reaping any material benefit. He'd accepted it, finding joy in service rather than wealth. But now, a part of him wondered: could he use this knowledge not just to help people, but to finally earn the kind of money that would allow him to live in comfort, perhaps even luxury? What if he could apply his hypnosis skills, now amplified by the science he'd learned from Dr. Kapoor's book, to earn a quick profit?

2. Life in the Mountainous Village

The village, though remote and small, had a charm all its own. Surrounded by lush green hills that rose steeply against the sky, the villagers lived amidst scenic beauty, but with limited resources. The people here were resilient and resourceful, taking what they needed from the land. Electricity was rare, with only a few houses equipped with solar-powered lights. The community depended on age-old methods of living, and people were bound to each other in close-knit ties, shaped by traditions and mutual trust.

Men and women alike toiled in the fields or took care of livestock, eking out their livelihoods with what little they had. Children roamed free, their laughter echoing through the narrow alleys, while the elderly sat on charpoys, weaving tales of olden days or guiding the younger generations with their wisdom.

This village was where Somesh had lived and served for most of his life. He was the community's healer, someone people looked to when illness or worry clouded their minds. Somesh's methods were a mix of herbal remedies and hypnosis, which he had learned from a distant uncle who practiced in the neighboring state. This uncle had taught him the art of using calm, repetitive words to ease people's minds, to guide them into a relaxed state where their bodies could heal.

3. The Healer's Art of Hypnosis

Somesh's skill with hypnosis was both respected and revered in the village. He was able to help people suffering from chronic pain, nightmares, or even long-buried emotional scars. People would come to him troubled, their minds heavy with worry, and he would calm them, helping them let go of their anxieties. His methods were gentle yet effective; he would speak in a soft, rhythmic tone, instructing his patients to close their eyes, breathe deeply, and focus on his voice. Gradually, their bodies would relax, their minds would settle, and the pain or worry that had plagued them would lift, if only for a time.

Somesh never charged for his services, and he lived simply, taking only what he needed. The villagers would occasionally offer him food, or help him repair his modest hut. His life was humble, yet fulfilling in its own way. But as he read Dr. Kapoor's book, a new possibility began to take shape in his mind.

4. The Power and Temptation of Knowledge

The sections on memory and hypnosis in Mysteries of Our Brain were particularly intriguing to Somesh. Dr. Kapoor described memory as a complex system, stored in various parts of the brain, each contributing to how we remember experiences, facts, and even emotions. Somesh had long known from experience that memories were deeply tied to a person's sense of identity and well-being. But now, with Dr. Kapoor's insights, he saw how memory could be manipulated—through hypnotic suggestion, people could be led to forget or recall events, even change how they felt about certain memories.

In one chapter, Dr. Kapoor described how hypnotic states could alter a person's perception, allowing them to experience vivid sensations or emotions as though they were real. Somesh began to understand that hypnosis was not merely a tool for healing—it was a way to access the very core of a person's mind. He realized that, in the right hands, this knowledge could be incredibly powerful.

And therein lay the temptation. Somesh began to think: if he could use these techniques to change people's memories or perceptions, couldn't he also influence them in other ways? Perhaps he could use his skills to gain favors, to make people more generous, or even to acquire wealth. The more he thought about it, the more he wondered: Could he finally turn his lifelong practice into a way to achieve the kind of life he had always dreamed of?

5. The Village's Silent Struggles and Somesh's Dilemma

Yet, Somesh's heart was torn. He knew the people in his village trusted him deeply. To them, he was not just a healer, but a friend, a confidant. People came to him not only for their physical pains but for comfort, for understanding. He had always been their protector, someone they looked up to. Could he betray that trust, even if it was for his own benefit?

As Somesh wrestled with his conscience, he wandered through the village, observing the lives of the people he had helped. He saw an elderly woman sitting on her doorstep, her back bent with age but her spirit still bright. He remembered how he had helped her sleep peacefully after her husband passed. He saw a young boy chasing a goat down a dusty path, laughing with joy, and remembered how he had cured the boy's recurrent nightmares. Each person he saw reminded him of the connection he had to this place, to these people.

But then, his mind drifted back to the dilapidated hut he lived in, to the patched clothes he wore, and the humble meals he ate each day. Surely, he thought, a person as skilled as he deserved more. Was it wrong to want a better life? And with Dr. Kapoor's insights now firmly in his grasp, he knew he had the means to achieve it.

6. The Crossroads of Choice

Somesh spent many sleepless nights, torn between his loyalty to the village and the possibility of using his newfound knowledge for personal gain. He saw two paths before him: he could continue as he always had, helping the villagers selflessly, or he could venture into a world where his skills would bring him wealth and perhaps even influence. He imagined himself moving to a city, setting up a clinic where people would pay handsomely for his services, where he could live in comfort and no longer worry about tomorrow.

But then, he thought about the village, about the people who depended on him, who trusted him with their lives and memories. He remembered how, despite his lack of wealth, he had always found fulfillment in helping others.

As dawn broke one morning, Somesh made his decision. He would continue to use his knowledge for good, to help his village without expecting anything in return. But he knew that the world outside was changing, and that one day, perhaps, his skills would be valued differently. Until then, he would hold fast to his principles, serving his village with the knowledge he had acquired, content in the knowledge that he was using his abilities for the betterment of others.

Observation

In the end, Somesh put Dr. Kapoor's book away, but the insights it had given him stayed with him. He knew that his understanding of hypnosis and memory would never be the same again. And though he remained in his humble hut, he carried within him a new appreciation for the power and responsibility that came with knowledge.

Chapter Eight - Malicious Ambition

1. Somesh's Dark Ambitions

As the night deepened in the quiet Himalayan village, Somesh was lost in thought. He had read Mysteries of Our Brain cover to cover, several times. He knew he needed more to turn his ideas into a reality. Dr. Kapoor's book had ignited a spark, yet it hinted at potentials that were just beyond his grasp. If only he could recruit Dr. Meera Kapoor—one of the celebrated scientists who had spoken at the book launch and an expert in the latest neural technologies, his plan might come to life.

Somesh began to outline his thoughts. His goal wasn't just to hypnotize individuals for small gains; he wanted to harness the power of hypnosis to manipulate memory in ways never before attempted. He had questions, endless questions, about what the combination of neuroscience and hypnosis could accomplish if it were paired with cutting-edge technology:

1. Could memories be manipulated and even reshaped through hypnosis? Somesh knew that hypnosis allowed him to influence how his subjects perceived events and even their emotions, but Dr.

Kapoor's book spoke of neuroplasticity and the brain's remarkable ability to adapt. Could he use this ability to actually alter a person's memory, embedding new thoughts or erasing painful ones?

2. Could signals from the brain be redirected and stored in an external device? Dr. Kapoor's work hinted at this possibility. If memories, emotions, and learned knowledge were essentially signals traveling between neurons, was it feasible to "extract" these signals and deposit them in a memory storage device? And if so, what sort of device could store such complex information? Could they use a specialized neural implant, or maybe even store memories in the cloud?

3. Could memories be retrieved and implanted into another brain? Somesh wondered: if they managed to store memories, could they then transmit them into another person's mind? This process would require either physical wiring or wireless transmission. But would the memories remain intact or degrade in some way? And could a recipient's mind be conditioned through hypnosis to "receive" foreign memories as though they were their own?

4. Who would control the data—the sender or the recipient? If they successfully implanted memories, could the original "owner" exert control over them, or would the memories merge seamlessly into the recipient's mind? Somesh feared that if memory manipulation went wrong, it could cause an identity crisis or even mental collapse in the subject.

5. What could go catastrophically wrong? He realized that manipulating memories could have severe consequences. If a person received someone else's memories, might they lose their sense of self? And if a powerful memory, such as a traumatic experience, were transferred, could it trigger psychological harm, or even physical reactions?

Driven by these questions, Somesh formulated a series of possible approaches. His knowledge in hypnosis was his strongest asset, but he understood he needed Dr. Kapoor's expertise in neuroscience to bring his vision to life.

2. Theories and Possibilities of Hypnotic Memory Manipulation and Reshaping Through Hypnosis

Dr. Kapoor's research had shown that the brain's memory centers, particularly the hippocampus and the prefrontal cortex, were highly susceptible to suggestion under hypnosis. This meant that, theoretically, memories could be "tagged" with false information or reinterpreted, essentially allowing Somesh to rewrite memories to suit his needs. With hypnosis, he could alter a subject's perception of events, changing how they recalled specific experiences, even leading them to believe in false memories.

By taking this a step further, Somesh imagined inducing memories of events that never occurred or erasing actual memories. This raised ethical concerns, as the line between reality and fabrication would blur.

But he recognized its potential for personal gain, allowing him to manipulate people's perceptions for financial advantage.

3. Brain Signal Diversion and External Memory Storage

One of Somesh's most ambitious ideas was to create an external device that could store memories outside the brain. Theoretically, if memories were electrical signals traveling through neurons, they could be intercepted and directed to an external medium. With Dr. Kapoor's guidance, he could explore possibilities like specialized chips, quantum storage devices, or cloud-based solutions.

To do this, they would need to attach electrodes to specific brain regions, capturing the unique electrical impulses associated with each memory. These impulses could then be converted into data stored digitally. Somesh imagined a device that would allow people to back up their memories, like a "memory hard drive." This idea opened the door to a whole new level of data storage—personal memories stored for potential retrieval at any time.

4.   Retrieving and Implanting Memories

The next challenge was to retrieve and implant memories from one brain to another. Hypothetically, if memories were stored as digital data, could they be downloaded and transmitted to another person? Somesh considered the mechanics of this process: could memories be imprinted directly into another brain's a neural pathway using hypnosis to guide the recipient's mind into "accepting" them?

Using physical wiring, the memory data could theoretically be transmitted directly into a brain, "rewiring" the recipient's neural pathways to integrate the new information. Alternatively, wireless transfer might also be possible with neural implants equipped with Wi-Fi capability. The recipient's mind would require a strong hypnotic suggestion to accept and interpret the foreign memories as their own. This process could allow an individual to learn new skills, languages, or even adopt new identities, if it worked without inducing mental chaos.

5. Control Over Memory Data: Sender or Recipient?

Somesh realized that if he succeeded in transferring memories, the question of control would become vital. Would the person who sent the memories retain some degree of control over them, or would the memories become fully absorbed by the recipient? If memories retained a link to the sender, it could allow for control, but this raised ethical and safety concerns. Could the sender manipulate the recipient remotely, or influence their thoughts?

Somesh feared that if control over memories were unclear, it could lead to severe consequences. For instance, the recipient might become overwhelmed or confused, unable to distinguish their real memories from the implanted ones. This loss of control could lead to split personalities, memory overlaps, or complete identity breakdown.

6. Potential Catastrophic Risks

Somesh pondered the catastrophic possibilities of memory manipulation. The human brain is fragile, and tampering with its memory centers could lead to disastrous results. If a person received traumatic memories, it could trigger intense emotional reactions, leading to mental disorders, phobias, or PTSD. A recipient's mind might struggle to process the implanted memories, leading to neural overload, psychosis, or even a vegetative state.

Moreover, if memory storage devices were hacked, a person's entire mind could be stolen or erased, leading to the risk of "mind theft." A criminal could potentially replace a person's real memories with false ones, effectively taking control of their identity. This horrifying prospect made Somesh hesitate, but the allure of wealth still tempted him.

7. Unanswered Questions and Ethical Dilemmas

As Somesh continued to contemplate his plan, more questions surfaced, each adding to the complexity of his scheme:

- Could certain memories be made inaccessible to the person, stored like "locked files" within the brain?

- If memories could be copied, could there be duplicates, allowing two people to share identical experiences?
- Could memories be edited or "enhanced," making them more vivid, powerful, or permanent?
- Could memory transfer technology be weaponized, implanting violent or destructive impulses in unsuspecting individuals?
- What would happen if the memory storage device malfunctioned, or if memories were corrupted during transfer?

The ethical implications grew increasingly complex. Manipulating memories meant interfering with a person's core identity, raising questions about consent, privacy, and autonomy. Somesh knew he would be crossing ethical boundaries, but the thought of the financial rewards—and the power he would wield clouded his judgment.

In the quiet of his village, Somesh decided to proceed. But he knew he needed Dr. Kapoor's collaboration, as her expertise could refine his raw, dangerous ideas into a sophisticated plan. If he could convince her to join him, they could combine the power of hypnosis with the latest advancements in neuroengineering to achieve feats of memory manipulation that were once mere science fiction. He envisioned a future where people's minds could be altered, controlled, and commodified a future in which he could be at the center of this powerful new domain.

But even as he sketched his plans, a sense of unease lingered. The line between knowledge and morality blurred, and Somesh wondered if his ambition might lead to unintended, possibly catastrophic consequences. Yet the potential for wealth and influence outweighed his doubts, and he resolved to push forward, no matter the risks.

Chapter Nine - Mysterious Emails

One late evening, Dr. Aryan Kapoor, a celebrated neuroscientist known for his groundbreaking work on memory, sat at his desk, browsing through emails. Among the messages, one with an intriguing subject line caught his attention: "Request for a Private Meeting: Hypnotic Healing and Brain Function Research". He opened the email, its unusual contents immediately piquing his interest.

The message was long, detailed, and almost uncomfortably earnest. The sender introduced himself as a "hypnotic healer" with a unique interest in understanding brain signaling and memory. He explained how his life had been dedicated to helping others through the art of hypnosis, but he felt his expertise had hit a barrier. Science, he claimed, was the missing piece that could help him advance beyond his current capabilities.

Dear Dr. Kapoor,

Allow me to introduce myself. I am a practitioner of hypnotic healing, someone who has spent years helping others confront and overcome emotional and mental obstacles. My methods, while rooted in traditional practice, are effective, and I have seen the profound impacts they have on those I treat. But I am reaching out to you because I feel that my understanding of the human mind has reached its limits. I have come to realize that I need the support of science to truly push the boundaries of what I can achieve.

I am seeking to meet with you personally because of your expertise in neuroscience. There is so much I wish to understand about how the brain stores, retrieves, and loses memories. My work in hypnosis has shown me that memory is fluid—sometimes it can be unlocked, and other times, it seems to disappear completely. I have seen people relive moments from years past with vivid detail and, in contrast, struggle to recall events just from yesterday. The brain, as I understand, is a vault of experiences and emotions. But where does it all go when people forget?

What interests me particularly are the following:

1. Short-term Memory – I am aware that short-term memory is fragile and easily disrupted. But what exactly happens when a short-term memory fails to transition to long-term memory? Why is some information immediately dismissed by the brain while other pieces are stored for a lifetime?

2. Total Memory Loss I have encountered individuals who have forgotten entire portions of their lives, not due to age but because of trauma or injury. Amnesia seems to occur without pattern why do some memories vanish while others remain intact? I am

intrigued by the mechanics of memory loss, as well as the potential for memory recovery.

3. Coma and Revival I have also had patients who have experienced comas, and upon revival, they often report feeling as though they've "lost time." Some struggle to reconnect with past memories, while others appear to have no recollection of the time spent in a coma. I am eager to understand what happens to memory during these prolonged states of unconsciousness.

4. After-effects on Memory Post-coma – This area fascinates me. Many patients have reported feeling "disconnected" or "fragmented" after waking from comas. I believe this experience is tied to memory and how the brain's signaling pathways are affected during the coma state. Is there a science behind this? If so, can it be manipulated to aid patients who suffer from memory disorders?

5. Mapping Memory Locations – My ultimate ambition is to understand how memories are mapped within the brain. I believe that with precise mapping, it might be possible to access specific memories or even help people retain vital information they are at risk of losing. I am aware that this is an advanced area of research, but I think there is untapped potential here.

6. Memory Transfer Processing – I understand this concept exists primarily in theoretical discussions, but I am captivated by the possibilities. Imagine if one could transfer memories from one person to another

or store them outside the human body. I believe such advancements could be a revolution in fields ranging from mental health to education.

In essence, I wish to know if it is possible to identify, isolate, and transfer memories or restore them for patients who are suffering from various forms of cognitive decline. I understand this sounds ambitious, perhaps even impossible, but I am convinced that the future of memory lies in bridging our minds with scientific technology.

Dr. Kapoor, I genuinely believe that there is immense potential in the cross-section of my field and your research. Together, we could unlock secrets about the human mind that have never been touched before. I am keenly aware of the ethical considerations this work would entail, but I assure you that my intentions are purely in the interest of helping people who suffer from memory-related issues. I wish to bring relief to those haunted by the inability to recall their lives or those who live in fear of memory deterioration.

If you are willing, I would deeply appreciate the opportunity to meet with you and learn from your extensive knowledge. I understand that your time is precious, and I would not make such a request if it were not for a deeply held belief that we can accomplish something profound together. I look forward to the possibility of your guidance and insights into this mysterious and crucial realm of human health.

Thank you for your time and consideration.

Sincerely,

A Hypnotic Healer

Dr. Kapoor sat back in his chair, absorbing the significance of this message. This healer's curiosity was relentless, his interest fueled by a desire to push the boundaries of conventional knowledge. The topics he mentioned were complex, involving not only neuroscience but also bioethics, psychology, and cutting-edge research.

Dr. Kapoor was no stranger to ambitious proposals, but something about this one unsettled him. The healer's questions about mapping memory locations and transferring memories were bold, touching on areas few in the scientific community dared to explore because of the risks involved. The potential misuse of such knowledge was enormous. If memory could be transferred or stored outside the brain, it opened the door to all kinds of abuses—memory theft, unauthorized memory implantation, even manipulation of a person's identity.

And yet, Dr. Kapoor couldn't ignore the healer's sincerity. The desire to help others was clear, and his understanding of memory-related issues was surprisingly comprehensive for someone without formal medical or scientific training. However, Dr. Kapoor knew better than to take these discussions lightly. Memory was not a simple process; it involved an intricate web of neurons, signaling pathways, and brain regions that worked together in a complex dance that was still not fully understood.

The healer's interest in memory transfer was particularly alarming. If memories could indeed be transferred or stored externally, it raised questions of control: who would own that memory? Would the recipient have autonomy, or would the sender maintain influence? These questions were not just scientific—they were deeply ethical, probing the very nature of identity and autonomy.

While he was curious to learn more about the healer's intentions, Dr. Kapoor knew he had to tread carefully. Sharing sensitive information about memory mapping or transfer could have unforeseen consequences, especially if the healer had a less altruistic purpose.

Dr. Kapoor decided he would meet with this healer but approach the conversation cautiously. He drafted a reply:

Dear Healer,

Thank you for reaching out and for your thoughtful message. I appreciate your deep interest in the science behind memory, cognition, and recovery. Your questions touch upon some of the most complex and profound aspects of neuroscience, and I commend you for your dedication to understanding them.

I would be open to an initial meeting to discuss general insights on brain function, memory processes, and neurological phenomena such as coma and memory mapping. However, please understand that certain areas, such as memory transfer and the mapping of specific memories, carry ethical considerations and are the subject of ongoing research and debate within the scientific community.

Given the nature of your questions, I believe it would be beneficial to meet in a neutral setting, where we can engage in a candid yet respectful conversation. If this arrangement suits you, please let me know.

Best regards,

Dr. Aryan Kapoor

As he hit "send," Dr. Kapoor knew this meeting could lead him into uncharted and potentially risky territory. Yet his scientific curiosity and a sense of responsibility to keep an eye on this mysterious healer compelled him forward. In the days that followed, Dr. Kapoor prepared himself for a conversation that might reshape not only his understanding of the brain but also the very boundaries of his ethical obligations as a scientist.

Dr. Aryan Kapoor barely had a moment to reflect on his reply before his inbox pinged with an immediate response from the mysterious hypnotic healer. The healer's message was detailed, probing deeper into the intricate and often elusive workings of the brain. This time, his questions were even more comprehensive, touching upon a wide range of neurological and psychological phenomena, revealing a mind driven by a relentless thirst for understanding the brain's every nuance.

Dear Dr. Kapoor,

Thank you for your prompt and considerate response. I truly appreciate your willingness to engage in what I believe to be a vital discussion on the mysteries of our brain. However, after further reflection and study, I find that there are additional aspects of human cognition and memory that I am eager to explore with you—areas that were perhaps underemphasized in your published work. I have outlined these areas below in hopes of shedding light on my ongoing research inquiries and aspirations.

1. Transfer of Signals between Body and Brain:

In my work, I have observed that hypnosis can sometimes influence physical sensations in parts of the body, seemingly by suggestion alone. This led me to wonder about the exact mechanisms behind how signals transfer from the brain to different body parts and vice versa. How does the brain interpret and process sensations from, say, an injury in the foot, and then send a response signal for pain or withdrawal? My understanding is that this involves a complex network of neurons, synapses, and neurotransmitters, but I am curious to learn more about how this signal processing can be influenced—or even redirected—by mental commands.

Furthermore, I would like to understand how these brain-body signals might be selectively controlled. For example, can one consciously inhibit pain signals to the brain, or is it possible to enhance certain sensory perceptions through external stimuli? If so, could such techniques be harnessed to aid patients with chronic pain or those undergoing rehabilitation after injury?

2. Emotional State of Mind When Recalling the Past:

Another area I'm particularly interested in is the emotional response associated with memory recall. Through hypnosis, I have seen people vividly relive moments from their past—sometimes joyful, other times traumatic. I'm curious to know what exactly occurs in the brain when a memory from decades ago evokes a powerful emotional response, as if it were happening in the present. For instance, why does recalling the death of a loved one, a past trauma, or even a moment of personal triumph still bring tears or laughter years later?

Does this emotional impact relate to specific structures in the brain, like the amygdala and hippocampus, which are responsible for emotion and memory? If so, how are these areas activated during memory recall, and why do certain memories retain such intense emotional power while others fade into insignificance? Understanding this could, I believe, have significant implications for treating trauma or unresolved emotional pain through methods such as hypnosis or therapeutic recall.

3. The Brain and Experiences of Fantasy:

I have often found that hypnosis can bring forward not only memories but also vivid fantasies, experiences that may never have actually happened yet feel remarkably real to the individual. This has led me to question the brain's role in creating fantasies, or "false memories," that feel real to the person experiencing them.

How does the brain differentiate between reality and imagination, or does it at all in certain states of mind? For instance, when someone visualizes a happy place or imagines a scenario during hypnosis, what is the brain doing to generate these seemingly tangible sensations and emotions? Are there specific areas or neurotransmitter activities that are involved in such "constructed realities"? And how might this insight be used therapeutically to help those suffering from anxiety, depression, or past trauma?

4. Mania and Phobia – Their Significance and Origin:

In my healing practice, I frequently encounter individuals with intense phobias or uncontrollable manias. I am eager to understand the brain's mechanisms that produce these conditions. Why does the brain react so powerfully to seemingly innocuous stimuli for some individuals, manifesting as irrational fears (phobias) or obsessive enthusiasm (manias)?

Are these responses solely psychological, or are they tied to specific brain structures and neurotransmitters? Do conditions like these signify an imbalance in certain neural pathways, or are they rooted in more profound memory associations or past traumas? I am curious about whether these responses can be modified or controlled through targeted brain stimulation or hypnotic suggestion, potentially offering relief to those affected.

5. Absent-mindedness and Memory Gaps:

I am also intrigued by the phenomenon of absent-mindedness or occasional memory lapses. Why does the brain, even a highly functional one, sometimes fail to retain recent memories or details? I'm aware that multitasking or distractions can interfere with memory encoding, but I'm curious if there is more to this.

For instance, can certain parts of the brain "overload," causing temporary lapses in memory, or is there a neurological explanation for why some people seem more prone to absent-mindedness than others? This could be especially relevant for individuals who report "zoning out" or experiencing momentary dissociation—what happens in the brain during these brief lapses of attention?

6. Hypnosis and the Brain's Functioning:

As a hypnotic healer, one of the most pressing questions I have is what happens in the brain during hypnosis itself. Why does the brain, under certain conditions, become more receptive to suggestion, and what areas of the brain are involved in this process? I understand that hypnosis likely involves the cerebral cortex, the thalamus, and the brain's limbic system, but I seek a clearer picture of how these areas interact to produce such a unique state of heightened suggestibility.

I am particularly interested in understanding why a hypnotized individual becomes so readily obedient to the commands of the hypnotist. Is it that the brain's frontal lobe, responsible for critical thinking and self-control, becomes inhibited, allowing deeper, instinctual regions to take precedence? How do brainwave patterns change during hypnosis, and could this state be measured or replicated under controlled circumstances?

7. Further Areas of Interest and Research in Memory Processing:

Lastly, I would like to inquire about any potential research on the transfer or external storage of memory. I am convinced that the future holds possibilities for memory manipulation and preservation, and that with a deeper understanding; it may be possible to create methods to transfer memory or safeguard it outside the brain. While I recognize the challenges of this area, I am curious whether you have insights on where such research might lead, and what ethical considerations we must bear in mind.

Are there any known experimental approaches to externally storing memory data, perhaps in a digital or electrochemical format? If a memory could indeed be mapped, transferred, and reintroduced into a different mind, would the memory remain genuine, or could it be altered or distorted by the new host's brain? This area, I believe, is not only scientifically fascinating but also holds potentially revolutionary applications in neurology, psychiatry, and even criminal rehabilitation.

Sincerely,

A Hypnotic Healer

As Dr. Kapoor read through the email, he was struck by the healer's perceptiveness and the profound implications of his questions. The healer was probing the deepest mysteries of the human mind, questions that had occupied scientists, philosophers, and physicians for centuries. Each inquiry hinted at an intersection between science, philosophy, and ethics—an exploration of human consciousness, identity, and the power of memory that went far beyond traditional medical knowledge.

These were topics that fascinated Dr. Kapoor as well, though he realized that delving into such matters required a level of responsibility and ethical restraint. The healer's curiosity was commendable, but some of his questions also carried potential risks if pursued without a thorough understanding of the complexities and ethical boundaries involved.

For now, Dr. Kapoor was left pondering the healer's message, recognizing that the journey they were about to embark upon might push the boundaries of current scientific understanding and ethical considerations alike.

The next email from the mysterious hypnotic healer arrived in Dr. Kapoor's inbox just as he was beginning to process the profound implications of their earlier correspondence. This time, the Dr. Kapoor receives another massage. Healer's message was direct yet unnerving, questioning the fundamental distinctions between intelligence and idiocy. Dr. Kapoor could feel his pulse quicken as he read each line, sensing a more profound curiosity lurking within the healer's inquiries—a curiosity that, while intellectually fascinating, seemed almost obsessively focused.

Dear Dr. Kapoor,

Once again, I am grateful for your responses to my questions, which have provided great insight into many aspects of brain function. Yet, there is still an area I would like to explore with your guidance—an area that probes the very essence of human cognition and potential. Specifically, I wish to understand the neurological differences between what society terms an "intelligent" person and an "idiot" or "dumb" person. While these words are harsh and, perhaps, simplistic, they represent real disparities in cognitive abilities, that are evident in every society and culture. My additional questions on this topic are as follows:

1. Neuroanatomical Basis of Intelligence and Idiocy:

What differentiates a highly intelligent mind from one that struggles with basic cognitive tasks? From your extensive research, is there a specific section of the brain or a unique configuration of neurons that governs intellectual abilities? And conversely, are there structural or functional differences in those who are deemed "idiots" by society? If so, I am curious to know which areas are involved—whether it is primarily the cerebral cortex, where advanced thinking occurs, or if intelligence relies on other interconnected regions and pathways.

2. The Cellular Orientation of Intelligence:

If intelligence can be linked to certain brain cells or neuron networks, what distinguishes the neurons of an intelligent person from those of a less cognitively adept individual? Is it the density of neurons, their interconnectivity, or the efficiency of neurotransmission? Are there any patterns or "structures" that scientists have observed that correlate directly with heightened intelligence?

My understanding is that intelligence involves both genetic and environmental factors, but I am intrigued to learn how these elements physically manifest within the brain's cellular architecture.

3. The Potential for Re-engineering Intelligence:

If there exists a structural foundation for intelligence, would it not be conceivable to "re-engineer" or alter that structure? For instance, could one manipulate or rearrange the neurons and their orientations to increase cognitive ability? Could brain training, stimulation, or even more invasive techniques help rewire the neural networks of a less intelligent mind? If so, what types of technologies or experimental research would be required to bring about such transformations?

I am particularly interested in whether it would be possible to enhance intelligence in individuals born with certain cognitive deficiencies or disorders. Could this re-orientation restore or even amplify their intellectual capabilities, allowing them to function at a higher cognitive level?

4. Research and Experiments for Neuro-enhancement:

To achieve an understanding of this re-engineering process, what kind of experiments would be necessary? Would it involve detailed brain mapping, live monitoring of neural activity, or specific neurological tests? Are there current experimental models—such as animal studies or brain-computer interfaces—that show promise in illuminating this field?

In particular, I am interested in the ethical implications of conducting such experiments. How could one safely study the potential manipulation of neuron orientation without causing harm to the subjects? What methodologies are employed to balance the drive for knowledge with the ethical responsibility toward those being studied?

Dr. Kapoor leaned back in his chair after finishing the letter, his mind buzzing with a mix of fascination and unease. The healer's questions delved into the very heart of intelligence and neuroplasticity, but there was a disquieting undertone to his inquiry—an urgency, even an obsession, with uncovering the secrets of human potential. These questions hinted at a desire not only to understand intelligence but potentially to control or augment it, raising ethical concerns.

For Dr. Kapoor, the healer's focus on "re-engineering" cognitive ability brought to mind the perils of manipulating such a delicate, intricate system. The healer seemed eager to push the boundaries of neuroscience into uncharted, ethically ambiguous territory, a place where human beings could be viewed as malleable collections of cells and neurons to be shaped or modified at will. As a neurosurgeon that had spent his career honoring the individuality of his patients, Dr. Kapoor was disturbed by the healer's apparent desire for knowledge without moral boundaries.

At the same time, he could not deny the scientific appeal of the healer's questions. The difference between a brilliant mind and a less cognitively adept one remained one of neuroscience's greatest mysteries. Although recent research had highlighted certain brain regions such as the prefrontal cortex and parietal lobes as crucial for intelligence, the interplay between genetics, neural connectivity, and environmental stimulation was still far from fully understood. The healer's questions touched on some of the field's most tantalizing—and ethically fraught—possibilities.

Dr. Kapoor's thoughts shifted to a darker question: why was the healer so focused on these specific topics?

His emails showed a growing interest in the anatomy and potential manipulation of the brain, particularly in ways that could fundamentally alter a person's identity and cognitive abilities. This was not typical of someone merely curious about the mind's workings; rather, it suggested a deeper, more personal motivation one that might not align with Dr. Kapoor's own principles of responsible scientific inquiry.

Despite his misgivings, Dr. Kapoor couldn't deny the healer's intellectual sophistication and passion for understanding the brain. But he also realized that he needed to approach this exchange with caution, weighing the potential impact of his knowledge before sharing any further insights.

With a wary yet intrigued mind, Dr. Kapoor decided to ponder his response carefully, aware that he was dealing with an individual whose intentions were not fully transparent, and whose vision of human potential might extend far beyond the bounds of traditional neuroscience.

Chapter Ten - The Meeting

In a sleek presidential suite of an upscale five-star hotel in the heart of a bustling metropolitan city, an unspoken tension filled the air. The room had been meticulously prepared, with every inch scrutinized for surveillance devices and all security gaps covered. It was the perfect hideaway for a clandestine meeting, a fortress disguised by luxury, prepared to host a conversation that could potentially shake the future of neuroscience and beyond.

Behind the drawn velvet curtains, the view overlooked the city, a shimmering sprawl of lights. Far below, traffic surged and honked, people moved through the night, blissfully unaware of the machinations unfolding at the heights above them. In the dimly lit room, shadows loomed, each belonging to a figure that had arrived under aliases, fake identities, and forged passports. Here, loyalty was fickle and only power and money held any sway.

At the center of this tense gathering was a figure known only as "The Broker." Shrouded in a charcoal suit, he sat at the head of a long mahogany table, exuding a sense of quiet menace. The Broker was well known in underworld circles as the intermediary between dark governments, criminal syndicates, and powerful rogue states. He was a man who thrived in the spaces between nations, a ghost with fingers on every continent, orchestrating deals that shaped conflicts and toppled leaders. Tonight, he was the conduit between the rogue nation in Southeast Asia and the underworld players who would execute their plans.

Across from The Broker sat a representative from the rogue state—a shadowy operative with a piercing gaze, known simply as "Mr. Tanaka." Tanaka was a high-ranking intelligence official, famed for his ruthlessness and intricate understanding of psychological warfare. His country's military and intelligence machinery operated under his command in total secrecy, pursuing whatever advances necessary to maintain the upper hand in an increasingly hostile global landscape. Tanaka understood all too well the potential Dr. Kapoor's research held for advancing their state's capabilities in mind control, memory manipulation, and neuroengineering.

On the opposite end of the table, a burly man with dark sunglasses and a scar that ran across his cheek sat silently, his massive frame exuding intimidation. This was Devraj Singh, an underworld don with vast influence over human trafficking, illegal arms, and contraband throughout South Asia. Singh was more accustomed to coercion and brute force than the silent diplomacy of espionage, but he had been brought in by The Broker for his tactical reach. His network of smugglers, enforcers, and local agents would be indispensable to carrying out this mission with discretion, ensuring that Kapoor's work could be secured without a trace.

As the final member of this clandestine group, the so-called "healer" sat to the side, uneasy and perspiring slightly. To him, this meeting marked an enormous leap. Only a month ago, he had believed he was a simple practitioner of hypnotherapy and healing techniques, with ambitions of personal gain. Yet, driven by a thirst for power and seduced by the ideas Dr. Kapoor's book presented, he found himself enmeshed in a plot he barely understood. The power brokers surrounding him were menacing and complex, and he could feel himself slipping, no longer fully in control of his own choices or intentions.

The Broker cleared his throat, drawing everyone's attention. "Gentlemen, we are all here tonight for a singular purpose: to ensure that Dr. Kapoor's groundbreaking research reaches the right hands—our hands. You all understand the stakes. This research on neuroengineering and memory manipulation could shift the balance of power as we know it. Imagine the potential if we could control not just actions, but thoughts, memories, and perceptions themselves."

Tanaka nodded his face expressionless. "In my country, we have long invested in psychological operations to influence masses. But until now, we have lacked the technology to enter the mind itself. Dr. Kapoor's work could give us that power."

Singh grunted, looking around at his partners. "This isn't just about science or tech. It's about the weaponization of the human mind. Once we have Kapoor's data, we don't just control individuals; we control entire populations. Compliance, obedience, there are no limits."

The healer, though out of his depth, couldn't resist asking, "What if Dr. Kapoor doesn't want to cooperate? He is a man of principles... This may not be easy."

The Broker gave a cold smile, revealing a flash of teeth. "Everyone has a price, healer. But if persuasion fails, we have... alternative methods." He gestured subtly toward Devraj Singh, whose reputation for getting "results" was well known.

As they continued to discuss their plans, Mr. Tanaka outlined the priorities of the rogue nation. "We need full access to Kapoor's understanding of neuroengineering—how the signals between the brain and body can be manipulated, stored, even transferred. If we can retrieve memories, alter emotions, control responses; our military capabilities will be unprecedented. Dr. Kapoor's research may hold the answer to all of this, but he must be... motivated to cooperate."

The healer glanced at Tanaka, curiosity and unease fighting within him. "If we're successful; what will happen then? How would this be used?"

Tanaka's expression remained inscrutable. "Imagine being able to create soldiers who feel no fear, who remember only what we want them to remember. Imagine being able to erase memories or suppress traumas of our enemies, to render them docile. Or conversely, to implant fear, loyalty, even artificial memories that serve our interests. Entire populations could be conditioned from birth. Kapoor's work could lead us to this."

The healer shuddered, imagining the full implications of such manipulation. He felt the chill of something vast and uncontainable—a force no human should wield. But he suppressed his fear, spurred on by visions of wealth and influence promised to him.

The Broker brought the discussion back to logistics. "Dr. Kapoor is a careful man, but not invincible. I have already arranged for surveillance of his movements, his communications, and his associates. Our plan will proceed in phases. First, we make contact. A formal invitation to meet with one of our people will be served under the pretense of a scientific conference. Once he is on neutral ground, we'll present him with our terms."

"If he refuses?" asked Singh with a grin, already relishing the possibility of forcing the doctor's hand.

The Broker replied with a chilling calmness, "Then we use pressure. Kapoor's family, his reputation, his legacy; all can be leveraged. We've done it before, and we will do it again if necessary."

The healer's anxiety deepened, but he remained silent. He was a man in too deep, pulled into a plan far beyond his initial intentions. He realized he was no longer just a healer with aspirations but a pawn in a far more elaborate and dangerous scheme.

As the final logistics were laid out, Mr. Tanaka nodded approvingly. "This operation will take precision. We have the resources, and we have the team. Once we secure Kapoor's research, there's no limit to what we can achieve."

The room was silent, the atmosphere thick with anticipation and danger. Outside, the hum of the city continued, oblivious to the chilling machinations unfolding above. As each man rose to leave, the Broker spoke one last time, looking directly at the healer. "Remember, healer, you wanted power. But know this: you are in this fully now. There's no turning back."

The healer nodded, feeling the full weight of his choices bearing down on him.

The day had arrived, casting a tense atmosphere over the upscale hotel in the city center. Inside, the quiet hum of luxurious decor mingled with a subtle buzz of anticipation, as if the building itself sensed the gravity of what was about to unfold. The grand lobby, decorated with chandeliers and intricate marble flooring, gleamed under the morning light that filtered in through expansive glass windows. Staff bustled with their usual calm efficiency, but beneath the polished surface, preparations were already underway.

In a suite on the ninth floor, two agents from the rogue nation had arrived early to finalize their arrangements. Their white Mercedes-Benz had slipped into the hotel's private entrance unnoticed by all but the most observant. The two men were dressed in sleek black suits, radiating the kind of understated authority that made people instinctively look away. Moving with an air of complete confidence, they bypassed the front desk, using a key card provided by a discreet contact within the hotel's management. They proceeded directly to their preferred suite, room 9001, a spot they'd used for other clandestine meetings; a place that held secrets from previous encounters.

They entered the suite, locking the door behind them. Inside, they checked the room meticulously, scanning for hidden devices and testing the hotel's private Wi-Fi network they had hijacked to avoid surveillance. One agent, a tall man with a scar just below his left eye, nodded approvingly as he adjusted his jacket, ensuring that a concealed pistol remained hidden yet within easy reach. This was a meeting they had prepared for extensively, and every detail was calculated to go without a hitch.

Meanwhile, outside the hotel, a sense of unease grew. Dr. Kapoor had made his way there under the careful watch of undercover police officers stationed throughout the building, blending seamlessly among hotel staff and guests. Kapoor knew he was about to enter a dangerous game, and the police had advised him to proceed with utmost caution. However, he hadn't shared the full extent of his research findings with law enforcement, keeping certain details hidden for reasons of both professional pride and national security.

Across town, the healer, known as "The Healer of the East," was on his way to the hotel, nervously clutching the invitation that had brought him here. Unlike the agents, his presence was not cloaked in confidence or indifference. He was anxious, unsure of how the meeting would go but compelled by an ambition he couldn't shake. His life had been spent practicing hypnotherapy and mind healing in his remote village, and though his curiosity about neuroscience was genuine, his thirst for power had driven him into treacherous territory. As he entered the hotel, his eyes darted around, absorbing the opulence that felt foreign and intimidating. He approached the reception desk with hesitation, showing his invitation to the staff member with a shaky hand.

"Ah, yes, sir," the receptionist said, casting a curious glance at the healer. She picked up the phone and made a brief call. Moments later, a suited hotel staff member arrived to escort him. "Please follow me to room 9001," the staff member said, his tone businesslike.

The healer swallowed, nodding slowly, and followed, clutching his satchel tightly as if it might shield him from what lay ahead. They made their way to the elevator, and as the doors slid shut, the healer could feel his heart pounding, the hum of the elevator intensifying his unease. Was he ready to meet the men he was aligning himself with, men who had far more influence and darker intentions than he'd anticipated?

Back in the lobby, Dr. Kapoor had just arrived. Stepping out of a modest sedan, he adjusted his glasses, taking in the hotel's imposing structure. He had been contacted by the healer initially, but something about the healer's recent questions and requests had alarmed him. His curiosity about brain functions, trauma, memory manipulation, and neural engineering had escalated into an obsession. Now, Kapoor sensed there was more to this meeting than an intellectual exchange. The healer seemed entangled with powers that would stop at nothing to exploit Kapoor's research.

Dr. Kapoor entered the lobby, and the receptionist immediately recognized him, a signal rehearsed earlier with the police. She approached with a smile, welcoming him warmly. "Dr. Kapoor, welcome," she said, gesturing towards a plush sofa. "Please have a seat. Someone will be here to meet you shortly."

Dr. Kapoor gave her a polite nod, settling down on the sofa and glancing around. The lobby's elegance contrasted sharply with the tension building within him. He checked his watch, each passing second heightening his awareness of the unseen eyes that might be monitoring his every move. He was in the middle of what he suspected was a web of complex, dangerous motives—yet he couldn't turn back now. The potential consequences for both him and his research, should it fall into the wrong hands, were too great to ignore.

Moments later, one of the agents emerged from the elevators. He was dressed in a gray suit, his movements precise and unhurried as he crossed the lobby. He approached Dr. Kapoor with a composed smile, extending a hand.

"Dr. Kapoor," the agent greeted his tone firm but polite. "I'll take you to the suite. Thank you for joining us."

Dr. Kapoor rose, offering a tentative handshake. As he followed the agent toward the elevators, he tried to read the man's expression, hoping to glean some hint of his intentions. Yet the agent remained inscrutable, his face betraying nothing.

They ascended in silence, the elevator's quiet hum seeming to echo Kapoor's growing sense of dread. He knew he was about to confront forces that operated beyond ethical lines, that sought to control knowledge without boundaries or consequences.

Meanwhile, on the ninth floor, the healer had been shown to room 9001 and was seated in a plush armchair, hands clasped as he awaited the arrival of the agents. His mind raced, filled with visions of the power he could wield if he mastered the secrets hidden in Dr. Kapoor's research. Though he had once been content as a healer in his village, the allure of greater influence had gradually overtaken him, clouding his judgment and drawing him into the orbit of men whose ambitions were far darker.

As the elevator doors slid open, the agent led Dr. Kapoor down a quiet, carpeted hallway. They stopped before the door to room 9001, and the agent knocked twice before entering. Inside, Dr. Kapoor's gaze landed first on the healer, who looked up in surprise, a flicker of recognition and nervous anticipation crossing his face.

The agent gestured for Dr. Kapoor to enter, closing the door behind him. Dr. Kapoor, believing the healer to be his intended contact, extended his hand with a cautious greeting. "Hello, Mr. Healer. How are you?"

The healer's face showed brief confusion, but he quickly recovered, nodding and clasping Dr. Kapoor's hand. Before the healer could respond, however, the door opened once more, and the two agents reentered, moving to stand on either side of the room with an air of authority.

The sudden change in atmosphere was palpable. Dr. Kapoor sensed that the men surrounding him were not merely interested in academic knowledge. These were men who would go to any lengths to acquire his work, individuals who saw knowledge as power and power as control. The air grew heavier, tinged with an unspoken tension that hung between them, thickening the silence.

One of the agents, a man with piercing eyes, finally broke the silence. "Dr. Kapoor, we have been anticipating this meeting. The healer here spoke highly of your expertise, and we believe you possess knowledge that could be... exceptionally valuable."

Dr. Kapoor felt a chill creep up his spine as he glanced at the healer, who looked away, his face a mixture of guilt and ambition. It was clear now that the healer had led him into a trap, aligning himself with those who had far more sinister intentions.

"What exactly is it you want from me?" Dr. Kapoor asked his voice steady but laced with tension.

The agent smirked, his tone cold and calculating. "What we want, Dr. Kapoor is simple. We need access to your research; complete access. Particularly in areas relating to neuroengineering, memory transfer, and brain signals. Your recent findings on the potential to store and manipulate memories could, shall we say, serve a much greater purpose."

Dr. Kapoor's mind raced as he weighed his options. He understood that the men before him had connections, resources, and influence far beyond his own. Yet he also knew that to hand over his work would be to unleash something dangerous, a power that could be exploited with catastrophic consequences.

The healer finally spoke up, his voice trembling slightly. "Dr. Kapoor, this is an opportunity; a chance to expand your research, to reach levels you never imagined. Imagine the possibilities!"

Dr. Kapoor turned to him, his expression one of disbelief and disappointment. "This isn't about possibilities, healer. This is about responsibility. You don't understand the risks."

Silence fell once more, and Dr. Kapoor could feel the agents' gaze hardening, their patience wearing thin. He realized he had to tread carefully, to buy time for the police stationed throughout the hotel to take action if the situation escalated.

As the tension in the room reached its peak, Dr. Kapoor felt a surge of resolve. He knew he was standing against forces that would stop at nothing, but he also knew he had a duty to protect the integrity of his work and prevent it from falling into the wrong hands. And he was prepared to do whatever it took to safeguard that trust.

Chapter Eleven - Mysterious Disappearance

The tension in the room had reached a suffocating peak, as the agents' demands grew more outrageous. Dr. Kapoor sat upright, his demeanor outwardly calm but his mind racing as he listened to their propositions—each more grotesque and morally unhinged than the last. The agents, who now sat closer, leaned in with controlled smiles, their eyes glinting with a steely confidence as they offered him a price: an exorbitant sum that would fund not only his research but a life of luxury, freedom from financial constraint, and the promise of unlimited resources.

"We can provide you with the best laboratories, Dr. Kapoor," said the agent with the scar, his voice low and persuasive. "Whatever you need—state-of-the-art equipment, live and deceased subjects, anything required to advance your work. Just imagine what you could achieve without boundaries or interference."

Dr. Kapoor shifted uncomfortably, keeping his expression neutral. He sensed they weren't accustomed to hearing refusal. Nevertheless, he gathered his composure and, with measured politeness, declined their offer. "I appreciate your interest in my work," he said diplomatically, "but my research isn't something I can share with just anyone. It's not about money or equipment—it's about purpose, responsibility."

The agents exchanged a brief look, their smiles fading slightly. The man with the scar leaned forward. "Think of the possibilities, Dr. Kapoor," he insisted. "We're offering you an unprecedented opportunity to conduct experiments most researchers can only dream of. Imagine live human volunteers, willing or otherwise, with no restrictions. You could open skulls, exchange sections of the brain, alter memory centers—reshape what it means to be human."

Dr. Kapoor's face tightened as he resisted the urge to react. This proposal, though laced with temptation, went against everything he valued. With a deep breath, he steadied his voice. "That isn't what I'm aiming for," he said firmly. "What you're asking is not research—it's exploitation."

"Exploitation?" repeated the second agent, chuckling softly. "Doctor, you're a scientist. Boundaries are an illusion created by those who lack vision. The work we propose could change the world, and you would be remembered as the one who unlocked the potential of the human mind."

Dr. Kapoor remained unmoved, his mind racing with the implications of their plan. "I understand you've come a long way," he said cautiously, "but I need time to think. This isn't a decision I can make lightly."

The agents exchanged another look, a silent acknowledgment that they would push no further—at least for now. "Of course, Doctor," the scarred agent said, a slight edge in his voice. "We wouldn't expect you to rush into something so... monumental." He nodded at the other agent, who picked up the teapot and poured steaming tea into a delicate porcelain cup, adding just a touch more than needed.

Dr. Kapoor accepted the cup and took a cautious sip, the warmth calming his nerves as he pondered his next move. But something felt wrong. A subtle drowsiness began to creep over him, his vision blurring as he took another sip. His mind, sharp and alert a moment ago, was slipping away like sand through his fingers. Realization struck too late—he had been drugged.

The agents watched as his eyelids drooped, his grip on the cup slackening. They exchanged satisfied nods as his body slumped forward, unconscious. Acting quickly, they stripped him of his clothes and signaled the healer, who had been waiting outside the suite, ready to take on a new role.

The healer entered the room, his hands shaking as he donned Dr. Kapoor's clothing. The agents observed him with clinical detachment, ensuring every detail was perfect. They adjusted his hair, fastened the cuffs, and even checked the positioning of Dr. Kapoor's watch. To the untrained eye, the healer could pass as Dr. Kapoor—a deception they intended to exploit fully.

With a knock, a hotel attendant appeared, pushing a wheelchair. He glanced at the slumped figure of Dr. Kapoor and the healer in the doctor's clothing but asked no questions. Trained in discretion, he proceeded to transfer Dr. Kapoor's limp form into the wheelchair with practiced ease. They rolled him to the service elevator, a route hidden from guests and reserved for staff, ensuring they avoided any suspicious eyes.

In the basement garage, a white Mercedes-Benz awaited. The driver and the attendant carefully lifted Dr. Kapoor's unconscious body into the back seat where, with the press of a button, the seat reclined and slid seamlessly into the car's trunk area. Hidden behind a false panel, the doctor was effectively invisible. The trunk closed with a soft click, and with another button, a new seat rose from below, filling the empty space in the back row as if nothing had changed.

Satisfied, the driver adjusted his mirror and waited as the healer, now posing as Dr. Kapoor, moved back to the lobby. The agents, their roles completed, exited through the hotel's side entrance, blending into the crowds that filled the streets, vanishing into the urban maze.

Back in the lobby, the healer settled into a sofa near the entrance, picking up a newspaper to complete his disguise. He glanced around occasionally, nervously checking his reflection in the gleaming glass fixtures to ensure he looked the part. For the next hour, he would remain in the hotel, giving the impression that Dr. Kapoor had lingered, unsuspecting of any impending threat.

An hour and a half passed. The police, who had been monitoring from nearby, began to worry when they received no signal from Dr. Kapoor. Several officers, dressed in plain clothes to blend in with the hotel's clientele, entered the lobby. They scanned the area and quickly spotted Dr. Kapoor sitting calmly on the sofa.

One officer, a tall man with a focused gaze, approached cautiously, calling Dr. Kapoor's name. The healer didn't react, his attention focused on the newspaper he held upside down, an uncharacteristic behavior that caught the officer's attention.

"Dr. Kapoor?" the officer repeated, more insistently this time.

The healer glanced up, his eyes filled with a hollow expression, not recognizing the officer. He mumbled incoherently; clearly nervous, his hands fumbling with the newspaper.

Another officer leaned forward, suspicious now. "Dr. Kapoor, we were supposed to meet with you," he said firmly, lowering his voice to avoid drawing attention. When there was no response, he quickly snatched the newspaper from the healer's hands, holding it up to reveal the back cover.

A collective gasp rippled through the officers as they took in the healer's features, his slight frame, and the faint trace of anxiety etched on his face. "This isn't Dr. Kapoor!" the officer exclaimed, his voice tight with alarm. "Who are you? Where is Dr. Kapoor?"

The healer stammered his voice weak as he struggled to keep up the facade. "I... I am... I mean, I.." he faltered, but the officers had already moved past him, their focus shifting from shock to swift action.

An officer rushed to the front desk, signaling the receptionist. "Search every corner of this hotel," he ordered, his tone urgent. "Dr. Kapoor is missing, and this man here has something to do with it."

Within minutes, the hotel became a scene of frantic investigation. Staff searched every suite, combing through hallways and staircases. They checked the service elevators, questioned every guest, and combed through security footage. The healer, sensing the walls closing in, watched the chaos with mounting fear.

As the officers scrambled, the healer seized his chance to escape. Under the cover of confusion, he slipped out through a side door. Outside, a car waited for him; another white sedan. The healer climbed in, casting one last look at the hotel's bustling entrance before disappearing into the maze of city streets, leaving no trace behind.

Inside, the police were left with an unsettling realization—Dr. Kapoor was gone, his whereabouts unknown. The healer, their only lead, had vanished without a trace. The officers regrouped, searching for any clue that might reveal what had happened, but the trail was cold.

The hotel manager, trembling under the scrutiny, approached the lead officer. "We're reviewing all security footage," he offered nervously, "but it's as if Dr. Kapoor was here one moment and then... gone."

The officer gritted his teeth, scanning the lobby with narrowed eyes. "This was orchestrated," he muttered, his voice filled with determination. "We're dealing with professionals. But they won't get away with this. They've made a mistake—someone will talk, someone will slip."

As the officers continued their search, their minds raced with questions: Where was Dr. Kapoor? How had he been spirited away so effortlessly? And what dark motives lay behind this intricate plot?

Chapter Twelve - The truth

The case had only just begun, and already, it had become a chilling mystery; one that would haunt the corridors of power and science alike as the police delved deeper into a world where the line between ambition and corruption had been crossed without a second thought.

The scene at the police station was tense, with the air filled with anticipation and a dash of hope. All senior officers were gathered, each looking at one another with a sense of urgency to crack the case of sudden abduction Dr. Kapoor from his hotel room. They had been deeply troubled by the mystery, each passing hour a reminder of their failure to protect the eminent doctor. Just then, the sound of footsteps approached, and a figure walked in, dressed exactly like Dr. Kapoor. The officers, their faces lighting up with relief, thought their ordeal was over. Was he back?

As the man took his seat across from the Commissioner and slowly removed his hat, gasps echoed around the room. The man looked exactly like Dr. Kapoor, but something was off in his expression, a blend of relief and dread. Finally, one of the officers stammered, "Dr. Kapoor, is that really you? How did you escape from the hotel? We thought you'd been abducted!"

Dr. Kapoor looked at each officer, allowing the commotion to subside before he spoke. His voice was low but carried a gravitas that made everyone lean in. "Look, Officers," he began, pausing as if choosing his words carefully, "when I came here to inform you about my meeting with the healer, I trusted that your team would take the necessary precautions. You assured me that your force would be on high alert, that I had nothing to worry about."

The Commissioner shifted uncomfortably in his seat, knowing there was some truth in what Dr. Kapoor was implying. Yet he had to defend his team. "Dr. Kapoor, we followed every protocol. But it appears that whoever is behind this abduction was well-organized, more resourceful than we anticipated."

Dr. Kapoor sighed, his face contorting with mixed emotions. "Perhaps; but my instincts told me to be wary, especially given the healer's controversial background. I couldn't shake the feeling that something was amiss, that our adversaries might have planned an ambush."

An officer interrupted, "Then why didn't you tell us? We could've increased the security presence, made sure nothing happened to you."

A look of resolve crossed Dr. Kapoor's face as he continued, "That's exactly why I decided to take an additional measure; one you would not have agreed to if I'd shared it. I contacted someone I could trust completely, someone who has experience in handling high-stakes cases."

The Commissioner's eyes narrowed immediately sensing the gravity in tone Dr. Kapoor. "Who are you talking about?"

"Detective Suborno Deb Barman", Dr. Kapoor replied, his voice unshakable.

The room filled with murmurs as officers exchanged glances. Suborno Deb Barman was a name they were well acquainted with an ex-police officer with an extraordinary reputation, a man whose mind was as sharp as a blade and whose methods were often unconventional but remarkably effective. The Commissioner leaned forward, a glint of interest and concern in his eyes.

"Suborno agreed to help?" he asked, his tone skeptical yet hopeful.

"Yes," Dr. Kapoor said. "He advised that it would be too risky for me to attend the meeting myself. He suggested we arrange for him to go instead, disguised as me. No one had seen the healer before, and nobody knew Suborno was in town. We believed it would be an effective swap."

"So, it was Suborno who went to the meeting in your place?" asked the Commissioner, his voice thick with disbelief.

Dr. Kapoor nodded solemnly. "Yes. Dressed in my clothes, carrying my belongings, he posed as me. We thought it would be a quick meeting, a chance to gather information. But now, I'm afraid I may have put my friend in terrible danger." His voice trembled slightly, a rare show of vulnerability that underscored the depth of his worry.

The officers sat in stunned silence, grappling with the revelation. It was a shocking twist that the person they were supposed to be protecting was not Dr. Kapoor at all but the renowned detective, Suborno Deb Barman. A man they had no idea was even in town was now in peril under their watch.

The Commissioner looked around, trying to gather his thoughts as the pieces of this puzzle settled into place. "So, you're telling us that the person they abducted was actually Suborno Deb Barman, and not you?"

"Precisely" Dr. Kapoor confirmed. "Suborno is now in the clutches of whoever orchestrated this, and they're under the false belief that they have Dr. Kapoor, the neuro scientist." He paused, visibly distressed. "I came here hoping you'd understand the severity of the situation and take immediate action. My friend risked his life to help me, and your forces have let him down."

The Commissioner held up a hand, trying to calm Dr. Kapoor; "Dr. Kapoor, we understand your distress, and we're as committed to finding him as you are. Detective Suborno is an exceptional individual—if anyone can manage under these circumstances, it's him. But we'll act fast. First, let's go over any clues we have, anything that could help us trace their movements."

An officer interjected, "Sir, we do have some CCTV footage from around the hotel. Perhaps we can track the vehicle that took him."

"Yes," the Commissioner agreed, "and we should reexamine any communications related to the healer and anyone who knew about the meeting location."

Dr. Kapoor shook his head. "Suborno was careful not to leave a trace, but if these people are as well-prepared as they appear, they might have anticipated every move. And, given Suborno's instincts, he may have left a subtle clue or signal for us to follow. I suggest we review everything with a fresh eye, especially any cryptic messages or patterns that seem out of place."

The officers exchanged nods, immediately springing into action. They divided the responsibilities, from combing through surveillance footage to analyzing Suborno's known contacts and reviewing reports from informants on suspicious activity around the hotel. The room buzzed with a renewed sense of urgency, every officer aware that time was running out.

Chapter Thirteen - The Clue

Hours passed, and the investigation grew intense. Leads came in and were pursued relentlessly, but none seemed to get them any closer to locating Suborno. Dr. Kapoor, pacing back and forth, began to fear the worst.

Finally, one of the officers burst into the room, holding a piece of paper. "Sir, I found something. A letter left under door of Dr. Kapoor's at the hotel room. It appears to be a message from Detective Suborno, written before he went to the meeting."

The Commissioner read the note aloud:

"If I am not back by dawn, it means the rabbit has led me into the lion's den. Seek the fox in the nearby forest. It knows the path well."

The officers exchanged confused looks. "What could this mean?" one of them asked.

Dr. Kapoor's face lit up with understanding. "The 'fox' refers to Suborno's former informant in the area, a man known for his resourcefulness. If anyone could lead us to Suborno's captors, it would be him. He knows the underground networks better than anyone."

Without hesitation, the Commissioner ordered a team to locate and bring in the informant. Time was of the essence, and Dr. Kapoor's renewed hope was palpable.

As dawn approached, the officers finally located the informant, who agreed to help them for a price. After some negotiation, he provided information that revealed a possible hideout location, a remote warehouse on the outskirts of the city. It was a place notorious for illegal dealings, a haven for people who operated outside the law. Even police avoid going to that area as adventurous police constables lost their lives. One officer is still in coma because of head injury sustained there.

In the early hours of the next morning the Commissioner and his team with Dr. Kapoor in tow, arrived at the location. They moved quietly, their weapons ready, and the Commissioner signaled for silence. The warehouse loomed dark and imposing, and there was a faint light coming from one of the windows.

With swift, coordinated movements, the officers stormed in, catching the abductors off guard. A fierce struggle ensued, but the officers were prepared, overpowering the men with precision. At last, in a corner of the dimly lit warehouse, they found Suborno, bound but unharmed. His eyes sparkled with relief and mischief as he looked up at the Commissioner.

"I knew you'd find me eventually," he said with a wry smile.

Dr. Kapoor rushed over, his face filled with gratitude and apology. "Suborno, I'm so sorry. I didn't mean for you to be caught in this mess."

Suborno chuckled. "No apologies necessary, old friend. It was quite an adventure. Besides, I knew you'd be here with the cavalry." He looked around at the officers and gave a respectful nod. "You all did well."

The Commissioner stepped forward, his voice stern but filled with respect. "Detective Suborno, we owe you a debt of gratitude. Dr. Kapoor, we promise we'll provide the protection you need from here on out. No more taking matters into your own hands."

Dr. Kapoor smiled, relieved and grateful. "Thank you, Commissioner. I'll trust your word this time."

As the morning light streamed in, the officers left the warehouse, each of them changed by the topsy-turvy events of the night. They had learned that in their line of work, sometimes the unexpected heroes are the ones who stand in the shadows, risking it all without any expectation of glory. As they drove back to the station; Dr. Kapoor and Detective Suborno exchanged a knowing glance, bound by an adventure that had strengthened their bond and changed them both forever.

The investigation into Dr. Kapoor's abduction and the master plan involving memory transfer technology had only grown deeper and more convoluted. Though Suborno Deb Barman and Dr. Kapoor were safe, it was clear that the case was far from over. The police's focus had now shifted to uncovering the mastermind behind the plot—a shadowy figure rumored to be after the memory-transfer technology for reasons yet to be revealed but clearly sinister. It was evident that an extensive network of agents, spies, and possibly international interests were involved, making it a high-stakes game for both Suborno and the police.

Chapter Fourteen - International linkage

After their daring rescue Dr. Kapoor and Suborno briefed the Commissioner on the bits of information they had gleaned. However, both of them agreed that the agents captured at the hotel knew very little about the broader plan. The police swiftly arranged for the court to remand the two agents, along with the healer, for fifteen days. In a highly guarded detention cell, they interrogated the trio for hours, hoping to break through their silence. Unfortunately, all three men seemed more than prepared to resist questioning, giving away nothing beyond basic, unhelpful responses. The officers tried psychological tactics, alternate questioning, and even subtle intimidation, but the prisoners remained tight-lipped.

Just as the investigation began to seem hopeless, an informant brought a critical piece of intelligence to the Commissioner. "A new man has entered the city, sir," he said, his voice low and urgent. "And he's been trying to get into contact with those three. He's even been seen near the police station."

The news brought a surge of energy to the room. It meant that whoever this man was, he had enough influence within the network to risk approaching their locked-up agents directly. They decided to use his desperation to their advantage, devising a careful trap. A trusted police officer was chosen for a special undercover assignment. Disguised as a low-ranking constable, he was posted at the detention center and allowed himself to become "acquainted" with the new visitor. Gradually, the constable let it slip that, with the right incentive; he might be persuaded to allow the visitor to meet with the detainees.

The plan worked. The visitor, an edgy, wiry man with piercing eyes, took the bait, slipping the "constable" a thick stack of bills as an entry fee. Late that night, in the cover of near silence, the officer arranged the meeting. He led the visitor through a maze of narrow, dimly lit corridors to the cell holding the two agents and the healer. Once inside, he set up the area for a supposed "private" meeting, all the while knowing that hidden cameras were capturing every movement, every word.

The visitor seemed displeased to see the healer among the detained agents and instructed the constable to "get rid of the man." Obediently, the officer led the healer to a different holding room through a connecting door, a move that was carefully planned to avoid arousing suspicion. The constable then quietly left the visitor with the remaining agents, returning to his position just outside the door. For five tense minutes, the visitor spoke to the detained agents in hushed tones, careful to mask his voice, but the hidden cameras picked up snippets of the conversation. They discussed something called "the transition" and exchanged codes that were impossible for the police to understand without further decryption. But it was enough to set the police on high alert.

Soon, the visitor signaled for the constable to return, paid him his due, and departed quickly. The constable watched from a distance as the man exited the station and hurried toward a black sedan parked discreetly in the shadows, with tinted windows and foreign license plates. The visitor climbed into the back, the door closing behind him with a soft click, and the car sped off into the night.

Unbeknownst to the visitor, his every move was monitored by the police. A fleet of two police cars followed him in the dark, their headlights dimmed to avoid detection. Above, a drone hovered at a distance, its high-resolution cameras trained on the sedan to provide constant visual updates to the officers in pursuit. They tracked the vehicle to the city airport, where the man quickly approached the ticket counter and purchased two tickets on an Air India flight departing for Beijing. The moment he purchased the tickets, an alert flashed in the police control room, confirming their suspicions of his next move. This was no ordinary operative; they were dealing with someone capable of accessing international resources and connections.

Given the urgency of the situation, the Commissioner coordinated with Air India's personnel, securing a plan to keep close surveillance on the man throughout his journey. Three officers from the force were chosen for a covert mission. They boarded the flight disguised as flight crew members, tasked with observing the man and his companion, documenting every movement and interaction on board.

The flight took off in the early hours of the morning. While the man sat in business class, sipping a drink and occasionally whispering to his associate, the officers kept a close watch from various positions, careful to blend in with the actual crew. By the time the plane landed in Beijing, the officers had gathered enough intelligence to confirm that their suspect was indeed an integral part of the mastermind's network.

Once they reached Beijing, a luxury sedan awaited for the man and his companion. This wasn't just any car; it bore a secret registration number, one commonly used by vehicles belonging to Chinese intelligence agencies. It was clear now that there were significant players involved, potentially supported by a foreign intelligence agency. The stakes had just escalated, and the Indian police team had to proceed cautiously.

An unmarked vehicle was also waiting for the undercover officers, courtesy of the Indian Embassy in Beijing. It took them directly to the embassy, where they briefed their contact on the situation and formulated a plan. Given the sensitive nature of the case and the involvement of Chinese intelligence, any overt action could risk diplomatic relations. The Indian officials decided to "observe and wait," agreeing it was too dangerous to provoke the foreign government without a more substantial grasp of the broader plot.

That night, the police team observed as the man and his companion were escorted by Chinese agents to a restricted facility in the city. Using their limited resources, the Indian team was able to track the location but was forced to remain at a safe distance, gathering whatever intelligence they could without detection.

The following morning, they filed a detailed report at the embassy, recounting the sequence of events and their suspicions. The report stated that the man had likely come to Beijing to initiate a critical step in the plan, possibly involving the exchange or transfer of technology or data related to memory manipulation. The police officers noted that the facility where they had been escorted was known for hosting covert scientific and technological experiments, a possible lead that would need to be explored in greater depth through diplomatic or intelligence channels.

Chapter Fifteen - Back in India

The Commissioner reviewed the team's report; he summoned a meeting with his officers along with Dr. Kapoor to discuss about their findings. Dr. Kapoor listened carefully, his face a mask of concern as he realized the full extent of what his abduction could have led to. The memory-transfer technology was a groundbreaking yet dangerous invention if it fell into the wrong hands, it could mean a new wave of psychological warfare. There were whispered rumors that certain countries had long been experimenting with cognitive technologies for espionage, and now Dr. Kapoor understood the gravity of the situation. His technology wasn't just a scientific innovation; it was a potential weapon.

Detective Suborno, seated across the room, remained silent as he took in the details. After a few minutes of quiet contemplation he spoke; his voice calm but carrying a decisive edge. "This is bigger than any of us anticipated. If we're up against a global network, we can't afford to be complacent. They're not just interested in memory transfer technology they're after control. And they'll stop at nothing to get it."

The Commissioner nodded, aware that this was a case unlike any they had encountered. The police would have to tread carefully, but he was determined not to let this matter slip through their grasp. "Suborno, Dr. Kapoor," he said, addressing both men, "I trust your instincts and insights on this. We need to stay ahead of them, anticipate their next move, and be prepared for any possible retaliation. Whatever it takes, we're going to bring this mastermind and his network to justice."

The team assembled, and each member was briefed on specific tasks to monitor any developments involving international agents, scientists, or diplomats with a particular focus on those arriving from or traveling to countries with known interests in cognitive technologies. They knew they couldn't let their guard down; the mastermind could still have operatives working within India, waiting to make another move.

In the days that followed, the police worked tirelessly, piecing together information, following leads, and scrutinizing every detail of the captured agents' pasts. Yet, the mastermind remained elusive, an invisible force pulling strings from the shadows.

Weeks passed, but the case remained unsolved, and the mastermind's motives only grew murkier. Suborno continued his investigations, moving quietly but with a sharp focus, always one step ahead of the others, determined to solve the puzzle. Each new piece of information revealed another layer of deception, leaving the team guessing about the mastermind's endgame.

But, as the days went by a feeling of anticipation hung over the case. Suborno knew this wasn't the end. Somewhere out there, the mastermind was waiting, possibly planning his next move. The threat of the memory-transfer technology falling into the wrong hands was too grave to ignore, and Suborno was resolved to bring this game of shadows and deceit to a close, no matter the cost. We have two agents who are their men. They will try to either eliminate them or rescue them. Suborno alerted the security personnel to remain ultra alert. Let's wait for their nex move.

With a sense of suspense, a mystery is lingering in the air. The journey wasn't over yet, and as Suborno looked into the distance he knew that the true confrontation with the mastermind was still ahead. For now, they would wait, gather strength, and prepare. The mastermind would make a mistake eventually, and when he did, Suborno and his team would be ready.

Part Two

Chapter Sixteen - Somewhere in southern India

As we dive into the next chapter of this unfolding story, we shift our focus to a mysterious, fortified building in an undisclosed location somewhere in the southern region of India. The imposing structure, set apart from the bustling towns and hidden within a vast expanse of greenery, is unlike any known facility. For the outside world, it doesn't even exist there are no signs, no maps, and no references in government records. The place is known only to a handful of high-ranking officials, trusted operatives and Dr. Kapoor only.

The building sits amidst 100 acres of agricultural land, designed with careful precision to look ordinary, just like any other rural settlement. From above, it's a patchwork of fields, lined with rows of crops that include wheat, rice, and a variety of vegetables. Interspersed among the crops are groves of fruit trees, nurtured meticulously by skilled horticulturists who appear to be civilian workers. They blend seamlessly with the landscape, going about their daily routines without a hint of anything unusual. But these aren't ordinary farmers they are a part of the meticulously crafted security apparatus for the secretive operations within.

The fortified building is surrounded by a seven-layer security system, though to an untrained eye, only the outermost layer is apparent. This outer layer is nothing more than a simple wire fence, painted green to blend with the vegetation, giving no impression of the extraordinary precautions in place. Each subsequent layer becomes progressively more complex, with strategically positioned motion detectors, infrared cameras, biometric checkpoints, and patrolling guards; most of whom are undercover agents trained to handle any threat. This level of security is typically associated with only the highest government facilities, hinting at the nature of the work conducted within.

The lab complex itself is housed in a three-story building of minimalist design, nestled in a secluded section of the grounds, hidden by an encircling layer of thick foliage and high walls. The walls are designed to resist both intrusions and eavesdropping, crafted from a special material to insulate against any form of electromagnetic interference or signal detection. The structure is built to withstand attacks and natural calamities, ensuring that whatever secrets lie within remain undisturbed by the outside world.

At the heart of this fortified estate houses laboratory of Dr. Kapoor. Though the world believes that Dr. Kapoor has long since retired from groundbreaking neurological research, only the privileged few in government circles know otherwise. This isolated laboratory has become the heart of his most ambitious and guarded project; a continuation of his earlier research on neural technologies, this time with an application that transcends typical scientific curiosity.

Outwardly, the lab maintains the appearance of a simple agricultural outpost. The daily operations here are supervised by a senior police officer holding the rank of Deputy Inspector General (DIG). Known only as Mr. Murthy, this officer is an enigmatic figure. To anyone observing from outside, Mr. Murthy is simply the supervisor of the expansive agricultural and horticultural operations. His quarters are located in a modest bungalow overlooking the garden village, a short distance from the main building. While he interacts with the local workers and oversees the agricultural routines, he never ventures close to the fortified building, and he never reveals his true purpose there.

The primary duties of this garden village are, in fact, more than just agricultural. The colony of security personnel—spread out over a series of quarters designed to resemble typical homes—plays a crucial role. Each individual, from the caretakers of the horticulture garden to the fishery experts, is a trained operative. Their true purpose is surveillance, maintaining a controlled environment where no detail goes unnoticed. The security protocol is such that anyone moving between layers of security must clear checkpoints and provide identification and biometric scans at every level.

As dusk falls each day, the security protocols become even stricter. Perimeter guards switch to thermal optics and night-vision equipment, patrolling the grounds in shifts. Patrol drones hover around the outer edges of the facility at random intervals, their surveillance extending across the vast fields and woods. There's no way in or out without passing through the watchful eyes of these guards. Any breach or unauthorized presence would be detected instantly, triggering an automatic lockdown of the entire facility.

Beyond the layered security lies Dr. Kapoor's sanctum the inner laboratory, outfitted with cutting-edge technology. Inside, the lab is a marvel of modern engineering and science. Each room is dedicated to a specific aspect of the research process, from neurological data collection to memory-transfer experiments. Rows of advanced computing equipment line the walls, connected to central data-processing hubs that analyze neural patterns. The air is heavy with the scent of sterilized equipment, a testament to the strict hygiene standards that preserve the pristine conditions essential for the sensitive work conducted here.

Dr. Kapoor himself spends most of his days in a sealed, high-tech research chamber within this lab, surrounded by intricate equipment that records brainwave data, monitors neurological reactions, and processes complex algorithms. His team consists of only a few handpicked scientists, each one meticulously vetted before being granted access. These individuals are among the brightest minds in neurological science, bound by oath and the knowledge that a single misstep could cost them their careers, or worse.

The core of Dr. Kapoor's research here is an innovation that could redefine human memory, cognition, and perception. This isn't simply an academic pursuit; it's a top-secret project that has potential applications in defense, intelligence, and national security. Dubbed "Project Mnemosyne" within the walls of this lab, the research is focused on the transference of memories and experiences from one individual to another; a technology that, if fully developed, could change the nature of intelligence-gathering, allowing operatives to "transfer" knowledge directly, bypassing conventional methods of training and education.

What remains unknown to the world—and perhaps even to Dr. Kapoor's own team is the true extent of his research. Dr. Kapoor has been experimenting with not only the transference of memory but also the enhancement of cognitive abilities. His experiments delve into the reconfiguration of neural pathways to amplify certain types of intelligence, strengthen memory recall, and even suppress traumatic experiences. This technology, however, comes with a high risk, as it requires deep understanding and manipulation of the human brain, which can be volatile and unpredictable.

The government of India, particularly its defense department, has high hopes for Project Mnemosyne. If successful, this technology could create a new breed of soldiers and intelligence operatives capable of near-instantaneous learning. Rather than spending years in training, operatives could undergo memory transfers, absorbing vital skills, language proficiency, and situational awareness within a matter of hours. This would not only give India a strategic advantage but would place the nation at the forefront of cognitive military science.

Chapter Seventeen - The brewing of doubt

However, such power attracts unwanted attention. Although the facility's location is a well-kept secret, international intelligence agencies have begun to suspect that Dr. Kapoor's "retirement" may be a cover for something more monumental. There have been sightings of foreign operatives in the nearby towns, their presence discreet but noticeable enough to trigger concern among the facility's security team. For this reason Dr. Kapoor has instructed Mr. Murthy to heighten the vigilance of his personnel and ensure that all data related to Project Mnemosyne is compartmentalized, accessible only to a select few, and transmitted through secure, encrypted channels.

Inside his personal quarters, Mr. Murthy maintains a surveillance setup that would rival even the most advanced intelligence agencies. Screens and monitors line his walls, displaying live feeds from every camera positioned across the compound. A hidden command center allows him to coordinate with his field operatives and track any disturbances, all while maintaining the appearance of a simple garden supervisor. His official role is a cover, a front to blend seamlessly into the facility's layout and prevent any outside suspicion from being aroused.

Unknown to all but a handful, there exists a secret underground level beneath the main laboratory building. Accessible only through a concealed elevator disguised as a storage room, this underground area houses the most sensitive aspects of Project Mnemosyne. Here, experiments are conducted on secure servers isolated from the internet, ensuring that data cannot be leaked or stolen through cyber attacks. The walls of this hidden chamber are reinforced with steel and insulated against electromagnetic interference, making it virtually impenetrable.

The underground level also houses a quarantine room, used for both physical and cognitive security. Here, any new discoveries or techniques are tested on artificial models before they are ever applied to human subjects. It is also a place where encrypted records of all experiments are kept, cataloging each breakthrough, failure, and hypothesis. Dr. Kapoor and Mr. Murthy have unrestricted access to this level, and they take great precautions to ensure that no unauthorized personnel ever approach it.

Back in the northern part of India, Dr. Kapoor's original neurological lab operates as a "decoy" facility, running routine research projects to keep up the appearance of an aging scientist involved in harmless, academic studies. Researchers there occasionally publish unremarkable findings in scientific journals, further reinforcing the image that Dr. Kapoor's best work is behind him. This facade helps maintain the secrecy of his true project, keeping prying eyes focused on mundane studies rather than the monumental advances happening in the fortified building far to the south.

The compound and all its occupants carry on with this illusion, day in and day out, the security team and the research personnel knowing that they are part of something that could reshape human capability. No one is permitted to speak about their work or the facility itself; they are sworn to absolute silence, under threat of severe consequences. For many of them, the stakes are clear—they are custodians of a technology that could tip the scales of global power. Even a single lapse in judgment could expose Dr. Kapoor's work to the outside world, endangering the facility and potentially the nation.

But Dr. Kapoor knows that keeping such a powerful tool under wraps indefinitely will be challenging. Already, whispers of his retirement and the groundbreaking work he once did have begun to attract unwanted attention. Though Project Mnemosyne is shrouded in secrecy, subtle leaks, speculative theories, and the curiosity of global intelligence agencies make Dr. Kapoor was aware that it's only a matter of time before they close in on his current activities.

Dr. Kapoor's fears are confirmed when a report arrives from Mr. Murthy's intelligence network: foreign operatives have been spotted in nearby towns, under various guises as tourists, researchers, and businesspeople. They seem to be probing, inquiring subtly into the area's unusual security arrangements and the facility's day-to-day operations. While Mr. Murthy and his team do their best to deflect attention by setting up misleading trails and cultivating decoy sites, the unusual amount of surveillance points to an imminent threat. Every individual in the compound is briefed to be cautious, watchful, and to avoid any interaction with outsiders.

At night, the underground chamber in Dr. Kapoor's laboratory becomes a hive of intense work and contemplation. He spends hours studying the brainwave patterns, charting the data, and refining the algorithms that underpin Project Mnemosyne. Despite the progress, he faces ethical dilemmas that weigh heavily on him. The very imagination of potential misuse of memory transfer technology should it fall into the wrong hands; troubles him deeply. Memories, skills, and even personality traits could be transferred or altered with precision but at what cost? As he pores over the data, he realizes the danger that lurks in creating a new breed of operatives who could be manipulated or controlled through implanted memories.

Dr. Kapoor is also aware that, beyond the Indian defense and intelligence community, private entities would pay astronomical sums for access to such technology. Corporations, powerful individuals, and even criminal organizations could exploit it for their own ends. His inner conflict grows as he balances his dedication to his country with the moral implications of his work. He knows he must be prepared for any possibility, including the need to dismantle the project if it becomes too dangerous.

The pressure mounts when one of his colleagues—an esteemed neuroscientist named Dr. Shankar—expresses reservations about the project's trajectory. Dr. Shankar is an ethical scientist, committed to using technology for the betterment of society. He's concerned about Project Mnemosyne's potential to infringe on individual autonomy and privacy, and he questions whether memory manipulation should be pursued at all. Confidentially, Dr. Kapoor and Dr. Shankar had discussed the ethical boundaries of their work. Dr. Kapoor reassures him, stating that the technology's primary purpose is national security and that it will be protected against abuse. However, the conversation planted a seed of doubt in Dr. Kapoor's mind and he finds himself increasingly troubled by his own justifications.

Meanwhile, Mr. Murthy, in his role as "supervisor" of the garden village, intensifies the security protocols. He arranges for additional surveillance cameras, employs more undercover operatives, and even enlists trained dogs to patrol the perimeter. His main goal is to prevent any foreign intelligence personnel from approaching the inner layers of the compound. However, he is equally cautious in how he manages his workforce, aware that imposing too many restrictions or protocols might arouse suspicion among the locals who occasionally visit the agricultural land or interact with the plain-clothed security officers.

The heightened security has an effect, and for a time, the foreign agents appear to retreat. But Dr. Kapoor and Mr. Murthy know that this quiet period is only temporary. They anticipate a renewed attempt, perhaps even more insidious, as these operatives gather intelligence from other sources to find an entry point into the fortified laboratory.

As days turn into weeks, Mr. Murthy's team intercepts encrypted messages that confirm their suspicions: a high-ranking foreign agent has been tasked with obtaining information on Project Mnemosyne, including its potential applications, technological specifications, and the identities of key personnel involved. This intelligence is shared with top officials in the Indian government, who instructed Dr. Kapoor to implement extreme countermeasures to protect the project.

Chapter Eighteen - Anticipation of the Project Mnemosyne

Dr. Kapoor decides to make a bold move. He instructs Mr. Murthy to arrange a decoy operation that will lead the foreign agents down a false trail, away from the main facility. The plan involves creating a series of fake documents, encrypted messages, and simulated lab equipment that suggest Project Mnemosyne is based in a different location, a "dummy" laboratory far from the southern region where they're actually working. Several team members are reassigned to the decoy lab to maintain the illusion, acting as if they are engaged in serious research activities. Mr. Murthy arranges for surveillance around the decoy site, anticipating that the foreign agents will be drawn there.

At the same time Dr. Kapoor continues his research with an even more focused intensity, knowing that time is running out. He begins pushing the limits of his technology, experimenting with memory transfer protocols that were previously theoretical. These experiments lead to breakthroughs in memory encoding, allowing Dr. Kapoor to, not only transfer memories but also modify them subtly. This development, while remarkable, frightens him. He realizes he now holds the power to not only implant memories but to alter them a responsibility that could lead to disastrous consequences if abused.

Just when it seems that the foreign agents have been successfully diverted to the decoy site, a new twist emerges. Dr. Shankar, who has been increasingly vocal about his ethical concerns, goes missing. At first, his absence is attributed to a personal emergency, but as days pass with no word from him, it becomes clear that something is amiss. Both Mr. Murthy and Dr. Kapoor had suspected that foreign operatives may have abducted him, hoping to extract information about Project Mnemosyne. The realization of Dr. Shankar's potential capture shakes Dr. Kapoor, as he knows his colleague holds detailed knowledge of their research and security protocols.

The situation is now at a critical juncture. Dr. Kapoor and Mr. Murthy convene a high-stakes meeting with their core team. They agree that all research data related to Project Mnemosyne will be moved to secure, offline storage, and portions of the project will be halted temporarily. Mr. Murthy increases the security presence, bringing in elite counterintelligence operatives to monitor for any additional breaches. They also establish a network of informants in nearby towns, instructed to report any suspicious activity.

In a decisive move Dr. Kapoor contacts his trusted friend, Detective Suborno Deb Barman, requesting his expertise in tracking down Dr. Shankar. Suborno, known for his remarkable deductive skills, immediately takes on the case. His arrival is a breath of fresh air for Dr. Kapoor, who trusts his friend Suborno's instincts implicitly; together, they devise a plan to trace Dr. Shankar's whereabouts, identifying potential safe houses and hideouts that the foreign agents might be using.

Suborno's investigation leads him to a remote village several miles from the decoy laboratory. Posing as a local tradesman, he gathers intelligence from villagers and uncovers a pattern of unusual activity, including the sighting of outsiders who match the descriptions of foreign agents. Through a combination of surveillance and analysis, Suborno finally locates Dr. Shankar, who is being held in a secluded farmhouse on the outskirts of the village. With Mr. Murthy's team's assistance, they launch a covert operation, rescuing Dr. Shankar without alerting the foreign operatives.

Back at the facility, Dr. Shankar is debriefed, revealing disturbing details about his capture. The foreign agents had interrogated him intensely, demanding information about Project Mnemosyne, but he had managed to hold his ground, misleading them with fabricated information about unrelated experiments. His courage under pressure renews the team's resolve to protect their work at all costs.

However, the ordeal leaves Dr. Kapoor with an unsettling sense of the risks, that Project Mnemosyne poses. After consulting with Suborno, he decides that the project must be put on indefinite hold until they can secure it fully. He personally oversees the dismantling of sensitive equipment, placing all research data in encrypted storage, and orders that key components of the project be disassembled and moved to undisclosed locations.

The second part concludes with Dr. Kapoor and Suborno sharing a quiet conversation in the dimly lit hallways of the laboratory. Dr. Kapoor, reflecting on the dangerous path he has walked, acknowledges that while Project Mnemosyne holds great promise, it could also bring catastrophic consequences if misused. The knowledge that the project exists, even in dormant form, will continue to be a magnet for those seeking to harness its potential for their own agendas.

Suborno, sensing his friend's conflict, reassures him that true wisdom lies in recognizing the limits of one's own power. With that Dr. Kapoor makes a final decision to lock away the core components of Project Mnemosyne, protecting it from the world until a time when its application can be controlled responsibly.

Chapter Nineteen - Lab goes down

But even as the lab goes silent, as equipment is powered down and doors are locked, a hint of suspense lingers in the air. Somewhere in the shadows, unknown forces remain vigilant, waiting for the slightest opening to strike again. Dr. Kapoor's work may be hidden for now, but its allure is far from extinguished. As days pass in the now quiet laboratory, the sense of foreboding only grows. Dr. Kapoor continues his routine in the fortified building, but his heart isn't at ease. Despite the intense security, the secrecy, and the multiple diversions set up by Mr. Murthy and his team, he knows that Project Mnemosyne is far from forgotten. Its potential impact on national security, the ethical risks, and the growing global interest weigh heavily on his mind.

Meanwhile, in the outside world, intelligence reports and foreign interests continue to bubble beneath the surface. There are whispers in diplomatic circles, theories circulating among scientists and defense analysts, and coded communications intercepted by Indian intelligence agencies. These messages suggest that some foreign entities are getting bolder, willing to take bigger risks to get closer to the technology. Indian authorities monitor these leads closely, knowing that the project's secrecy is increasingly fragile.

Within the fortified compound the officers and scientists working with Dr. Kapoor maintain a heightened level of vigilance. Security protocols have become even stricter: random ID checks, patrols that change routes nightly and undercover officers who blend into the horticulture and fisheries teams. Mr. Murthy, known for his unyielding discipline, continues to run the facility like a finely-tuned machine. To onlookers, the village seems like a normal agricultural and research site, but every officer is trained to react at a moment's notice.

Despite the outward calm Dr. Kapoor's concerns don't wane. He has witnessed firsthand how power can corrupt even the most well-intentioned projects. Project Mnemosyne, with its unprecedented capacity to manipulate memory, could alter the course of individuals' lives, destabilize societies, and even compromise national security if misused. His decision to shelve it temporarily was only the beginning of a much larger question: should he destroy it altogether?

This ethical dilemma leads Dr. Kapoor into a sleepless night of deliberation. With a final resolution in mind, he calls Suborno for one last meeting. The two friends, seated across from each other in a secure, soundproofed room deep within the facility, discuss the future of Project Mnemosyne.

"Suborno," Dr. Kapoor begins his voice heavy with the weight of his decision. "If something were to happen to me or if I were coerced into revealing the secrets of this technology, the consequences could be catastrophic. We can't let this fall into the wrong hands."

Suborno listens carefully, reading the resolve in Dr. Kapoor's eyes; "What are you proposing, Dr. Kapoor?"

With a steady voice Dr. Kapoor reveals his plan: he wants to erase all documentation of the project, destroy the prototype equipment, and scatter the encrypted data across multiple locations around the world, places where only a few trusted allies would know to look. Only under an extreme threat to national security would the data be retrieved, pieced together, and redeployed. Dr. Kapoor is willing to take the extreme step of erasing his own memories of the project, using Mnemosyne on himself to ensure the technology stays buried until a time when the world is prepared to handle it responsibly.

Suborno is visibly shaken by the plan. He knows the magnitude of Dr. Kapoor's work, the years of dedication, and the risks involved. But he also understands the noble sacrifice his friend is prepared to make.

"Are you certain this is the path you want to take?" Suborno asks, his voice barely a whisper.

Dr. Kapoor nods, his resolve unwavering. "Yes, this is the only way to protect what we've built, to keep it safe from those who would abuse it. I trust you, Suborno. If anything were to happen, you know the contingency plans."

As dawn breaks, the preparations begin. Under the guise of a routine maintenance procedure, the facility's core systems are reconfigured. Over the next several days, all data related to Project Mnemosyne is fragmented, encrypted, and dispersed through a network of secure digital storage locations worldwide. Each piece of data is given a unique encryption key that only Dr. Kapoor and Suborno know, with backup codes entrusted to Mr. Murthy in the event of an emergency. Apart from them, a very senior person from defence department who though could not use the code himself but he had the power to activate the code for using it through the repository of the secret data bank.

Once the data is safely fragmented, Dr. Kapoor personally oversees the dismantling of the prototype equipment. He watches with mixed emotions as the hardware is taken apart piece by piece, each component destroyed or concealed within innocuous equipment that will be distributed to various research facilities as decoys. In one final step, the remaining researchers are reassigned to different projects, unaware that they've just contributed to the hiding of one of the world's most advanced technologies.

With everything set, Dr. Kapoor is left with one final step: using the Mnemosyne technology on himself. Suborno insists on being present, and Mr. Murthy prepares the team to handle any potential complications. Dr. Kapoor sits alone in his lab, with only Suborno at his side, and prepares to initiate the memory modification procedure.

"Goodbye, Suborno," Dr. Kapoor says quietly, his eyes filled with gratitude. "This may be the last time I remember any of this. If it all goes as planned, Mnemosyne will be forgotten by me, by this facility, by everyone who might misuse it."

Dr. Kapoor closes his eyes; Suborno initiates the memory transfer device, erasing all traces of Project Mnemosyne from mind of Dr. Kapoor. The process is silent, peaceful, and almost surreal. Dr. Kapoor emerges with no recollection of the project, his mind clear but changed; unaware of the technological marvel he has hidden from the world.

With the completion of the procedure Dr. Kapoor retires to his quiet life in the village, unaware of the massive technological advancement he once spearheaded. The compound operates as a normal research site, and only a handful of trusted officials know the truth of what lies hidden in fragments around the globe.

The story ends with Suborno watching Dr. Kapoor from afar, reflecting on the courage it took for his friend to protect the future at the cost of his own memories. He knows the decision was the right one, but he can't shake the feeling that someday, someone may try to resurrect Project Mnemosyne. And when that day comes, the world will face a choice: to use or to abuse the knowledge Dr. Kapoor once held.

For now, though, Project Mnemosyne remains dormant, its secrets scattered, hidden, and waiting. And as the last piece of equipment powers down in the lab; a quiet calm settles over the fortified building; a calm that belies the potential storm brewing just beneath the surface.

Chapter Twenty - Alarm Bell calling

Months pass quietly at the fortified facility, now reduced to a seemingly ordinary research center. Dr. Kapoor's life has returned to simplicity. He oversees daily operations, unaware of the extraordinary knowledge he once held. He works with younger scientists, teaching them basic neurology and ethics, and spending time in the gardens. The villagers around the compound have come to know him as a wise, gentle man, unaware of the monumental secrets hidden in his past.

Suborno, meanwhile, has returned to his own life, but he remains vigilant. Though the project is dormant, he's well aware that a secret like Project Mnemosyne cannot stay hidden forever. A breakthrough like memory transfer and alteration technology is too powerful and tempting. He knows that even though Dr. Kapoor erased his own memories others still harbor ambitions of harnessing that power for their own purposes. Suborno's instincts tell him it's only a matter of time before those forces resurface, looking for the fragmented pieces of Mnemosyne.

One evening, Suborno receives a message through a secure channel, marked "URGENT." It's from Mr.

Murthy, the head of security at the fortified facility. The message is short but alarming:

"Unusual activity detected around former laboratory Dr. Kapoor; multiple breaches attempted in the data archives. Potentially foreign agents involved; request immediate backup."

The message confirms Suborno's worst fears: someone has rediscovered Mnemosyne's existence and is actively seeking it out. If the fragmented pieces of the project fall into the wrong hands, the repercussions could be catastrophic—not just for Dr. Kapoor, but for anyone whose memories or identities could be manipulated. Mnemosyne could be turned into a weapon of psychological warfare.

Without hesitation, Suborno assembles a small team of trusted officers, experts in counterintelligence and cyber-security. They head to the facility in the dead of night, planning their response carefully. Once they arrive, Mr. Murthy briefs them on the situation: hackers had breached certain levels of the digital security network, attempting to access files that, to most people, wouldn't appear significant. But to someone with knowledge of Project Mnemosyne, these fragmented bits of data could be the first step toward reconstructing the entire project.

Suborno realizes they need to act quickly to trace the origins of these attacks. The encrypted fragments were supposed to be hidden across multiple, seemingly unrelated servers worldwide. If someone has already found Dr. Kapoor's former laboratory files, it means they may be closer to discovering other parts of the project. He orders a full investigation into recent internet activity, focusing on any patterns suggesting coordinated access attempts across secure networks in other countries.

Days go by, and Suborno's team uncovers a disturbing pattern: the breaches have ties to multiple international networks, including some suspicious connections to shadow organizations linked to foreign intelligence services. It's clear that the technology is not only being pursued by rogue scientists but also by state-sponsored actors who understand its potential impact.

Chapter Twenty One - A Visitor

Meanwhile back at the fortified facility, Dr. Kapoor remains unaware of the brewing storm. To him, life continues as usual, with the rhythms of gardening and teaching filling his days. However, a new visitor arrives; a young woman claiming to be a student interested in neurology. She appears eager, inquisitive, and polite, winning Dr. Kapoor's trust with her thoughtful questions and quick learning. But as the days go on, she begins subtly probing him for information, particularly regarding his past research.

Unbeknownst to Dr. Kapoor, this young woman is a skilled agent, sent by one of the shadow organizations tracking Project Mnemosyne. Her mission is to assess whether Dr. Kapoor has retained any memory of the technology and, if possible, locate any hidden files or physical remnants of the project.

Suborno, sensing the urgency of the situation, decides it's time to visit the facility in person. He knows that if foreign agents have infiltrated Dr. Kapoor's quiet life, the situation could spiral out of control quickly. Disguised as a researcher, Suborno returns to the compound and begins a covert investigation. He soon notices the young woman, whose behavior doesn't quite match that of an ordinary student.

After observing her movements, Suborno sets a trap, arranging a meeting under the guise of a research seminar. In a private room, Suborno confronts her, revealing his knowledge of her true identity and demanding to know her purpose. The agent, caught off guard, tries to evade him but quickly realizes she's cornered. She finally admits her affiliation with a foreign intelligence agency, though she refuses to disclose her objectives.

Determined to get more information, Suborno places her under surveillance, instructing his team to track all of her communications. It doesn't take long before they intercept a coded message revealing her mission: she had been sent to ascertain the existence of Project Mnemosyne and report any findings to her agency.

Suborno's worst fears are confirmed: the world knows, or at least suspects, that Mnemosyne exists. With the stakes now higher than ever, Suborno consults with Mr. Murthy and the rest of his team to decide on the next steps. They agree that they must do whatever it takes to prevent any unauthorized access to the project's fragments and ensure that Dr. Kapoor remains protected.

In a final, decisive move, Suborno devises a plan to fake the complete destruction of all remaining Mnemosyne-related data. They would plant decoy files in Dr. Kapoor's former laboratory and release a controlled "leak" suggesting that a laboratory accident had rendered the data unrecoverable. This maneuver would give the impression that Mnemosyne no longer exists, effectively ending the hunt for the technology.

The plan is executed with meticulous precision. News reports are carefully crafted to suggest that an incident occurred, resulting in a total data loss. The laboratory is temporarily shut down, and the story is circulated through international intelligence channels, effectively planting the idea that Mnemosyne was never fully realized and is now lost to history.

The world's attention begins to fade, and for the first time in months, Suborno feels a sense of relief. He knows they've managed to shield fortified compound of Dr. Kapoor. The Project Mnemosyne was protected from the relentless forces that sought it. The fragmented data remains hidden, scattered across multiple locations, accessible only under the strictest conditions and only in a national emergency.

Back at the compound, life returns to its tranquil pace. Dr. Kapoor continues his quiet life, blissfully unaware of the global chase surrounding him. Suborno bids his friend farewell, leaving him to his peaceful routine. As he exits the facility, Suborno is filled with both satisfaction and a lingering sense of vigilance. He knows that while they've successfully deflected attention for now, the potential for Mnemosyne's rediscovery will always loom in the shadows.

With a final look at the fortified facility, Suborno resolves to remain on guard, prepared for the day when the world's curiosity about memory manipulation technology reignites. He knows the power of Mnemosyne, and he's prepared to protect its secrets until the world is truly ready to handle it responsibly.

And as he drives away, he reflects on the delicate balance between innovation and responsibility, aware that the legacy of Project Mnemosyne will continue, hidden yet eternal, as long as its mysteries remain untapped. The world may have forgotten it for now, but its dormant potential lives on, waiting—perhaps for a new era, a new generation, or even a new champion to rediscover it in a time of greater wisdom.

As Suborno leaves the fortified facility, the night air feels heavy, almost charged, as though the secrets buried there might one day find their way back to the world. He knows that he has done everything possible to protect Dr. Kapoor and his hidden technology. the extension of his research would help countless lives that could be impacted by memory manipulation.

Months turn into years, and the quiet around Project Mnemosyne seems almost too good to be true. The world has moved on, and Dr. Kapoor's life has become something of a legend among the few who once knew him personally. His former students and associates speak of his brilliance and vision, but even they believe that his research on memory transfer was never fully realized. In the official records, Project Mnemosyne has been written off as a myth, an ambitious endeavor that never reached its full potential.

However, the story does not end here. Across the world, quiet whispers have begun to resurface in clandestine circles, rumors about a memory-altering technology that was once on the verge of completion. The technology, some say, has the potential to reshape histories, alter perceptions, and even rewrite identities. These whispers are vague and fragmented, but they have begun to attract the interest of a new generation of intelligence agencies, scientific radicals, and tech magnates with ambitious and often unscrupulous goals.

One such figure is an enigmatic tech mogul named Rajan Venkatesh. Known for his obsession with cutting-edge artificial intelligence and biotechnology, Venkatesh is rumored to have access to resources that could rival those of any government. He has been following these whispers about Mnemosyne and is determined to track down its origins. Unlike previous pursuers, he believes in subtlety and knows that brute force and direct infiltration attempts will only alert those who guard the secrets he seeks. Instead, he operates from the shadows, creating a network of informants, ex-agents, and hackers to piece together the fragments of Mnemosyne's existence.

Venkatesh's reach eventually leads him to one name: Dr. Kapoor. Through a combination of leaked documents and advanced data mining, he uncovers references to the neurologist and his former laboratory, as well as certain "incidents" that suggest a cover-up orchestrated by Indian intelligence. Intrigued and undeterred, Venkatesh begins to devise a plan to locate and approach Dr. Kapoor, convinced that the aging scientist might hold some clue, however deeply hidden.

Meanwhile, Suborno's life has returned to a semblance of normalcy. He has continued solving cases, each one unique and challenging, yet none carrying the weight of Project Mnemosyne. But one evening, he receives a cryptic message from an unknown source, simply stating, "He's looking for Mnemosyne. You must act." The message includes coordinates for a location in southern India, close to where Dr. Kapoor's fortified facility is hidden.

Suborno's instincts sharpen. He immediately suspects that someone is targeting Dr. Aryan Kapoor again and that the project, once thought buried, is in danger of being unearthed. Determined to protect both his friend and the legacy of Mnemosyne, he calls upon a select team of trusted operatives, prepared to confront whatever force has reawakened this hidden threat.

As he arrives near the facility, he meets with Mr. Murthy, who has been monitoring strange activities in the vicinity. Surveillance reports indicate unusual drone sightings, suspicious new residents in the nearby village, and an increase in encrypted communications originating from unknown sources. It is clear that something—or someone—is closing in.

Chapter Twenty Two - Lure and Plan

Together, Suborno and Murthy hatch a plan. They will allow Venkatesh's operatives to enter the facility, luring them into a secure area specially designed for containment. The trap is set: the secure zone appears to be an innocuous storage area within the facility, but it is equipped with hidden cameras, silent alarms, and reinforced walls. Once inside, the intruders would unknowingly trigger a series of automated locks, capturing them in place.

The day arrives, and Suborno and his team lie in wait. Just before midnight, they observe a group of four individuals attempting to breach the facility's outer perimeter, led by none other than Venkatesh himself. The intruders proceed with precision, bypassing the first few layers of security, clearly well-prepared and trained for the task. Their confidence grows as they draw closer to the central compound, unaware that they are being led into an elaborate trap.

Finally, the moment of reckoning arrives. As they enter the containment zone, Suborno gives the signal, and the doors lock in place. Venkatesh and his team realize too late that they've been ensnared. Suborno appears on a monitor within the containment area, addressing them directly.

"Mr. Venkatesh," he says, his voice calm but steely. "I commend your resourcefulness. You've managed to come closer to Mnemosyne than anyone else before you. But know this: this technology was buried for a reason. Its potential for harm far outweighs any possible benefit, and I will not allow it to fall into the wrong hands."

Venkatesh, realizing the situation, attempts to negotiate, arguing that Mnemosyne could revolutionize the fields of medicine and memory treatment. He speaks passionately about his vision for a future where memories can be preserved, where Alzheimer's and dementia could be eliminated. But Suborno remains unmoved, recognizing the underlying ambition and disregard for ethical boundaries.

"You see this as a tool for progress, Mr. Venkatesh," Suborno replies. "But without restraint, it would only become a weapon, one that could reshape minds and manipulate truths. Mnemosyne was never meant for the world you envision."

With no other options, Venkatesh and his team are taken into custody. However, Suborno knows that this is only a temporary victory. He understands that as long as Mnemosyne's legacy exists, there will be those who seek it, and it will continue to cast a shadow over Dr. Kapoor and the countless lives potentially affected by it.

Suborno meets with government officials, urging them to dismantle all remaining Mnemosyne-related files and reclassify research of Dr. Kapoor as permanently sealed project. He insists on stricter security protocols, knowing that vigilance will be their only defense against those who would try again. With heavy hearts, the officials agree, taking measures to ensure that Mnemosyne will be confined to history, its secrets kept safe from prying eyes.

For Dr. Kapoor, life continues peacefully. Suborno chooses not to reveal any of these events to his old friend, allowing him the tranquility he has earned. The fortified facility becomes a place of simple research and agriculture, blending into the landscape, forgotten by all but a select few.

And so, Mnemosyne fades once more into obscurity, its mysteries untouched, waiting for a world wiser and more responsible—if such a world ever exists to rediscover it.

Though Mnemosyne is secured for now, Suborno feels a lingering unease. The confrontation with Venkatesh, while a victory, revealed just how vulnerable the project remained, even after extensive precautions. The allure of its secrets is too powerful; the promise of manipulating memories, controlling minds, and altering realities will always attract the ambitious, the ruthless, and the desperate.

Weeks pass, and Suborno returns to his regular life, focusing on solving high-stakes cases and restoring order where others see only chaos. Yet, in the quiet moments, he finds himself haunted by Mnemosyne's potential its power to rewrite memories and change a person's perception, a power far more dangerous than any weapon. Could the world ever be trusted with such technology? Or would it inevitably fall into hands like Venkatesh's, ready to exploit it for influence, control, or even domination?

One late evening, Suborno receives a package with no return address. Inside are a small, nondescript USB drive and a note written in a firm, meticulous hand: "What you destroyed was only the beginning. The world's fascination with memory manipulation has only just begun."

Suborno's instincts tell him this is no idle threat. Someone else, possibly a group or an entire network, is out there, just as determined as Venkatesh to obtain Mnemosyne's secrets or recreate it from scratch. The USB drive, he realizes, is a symbol, an invitation, a challenge, and a warning all at once.

Hesitating only for a moment, he connects the drive to an isolated, offline laptop. Instantly, a series of encrypted files flash on the screen. They contain research notes on memory transfer, brain mapping, and even speculative theories about augmenting memories with artificial intelligence. The sophistication of the work suggests that it is not the effort of a single individual but the collaboration of several scientists, perhaps backed by powerful, hidden players.

As he scans the contents, Suborno feels a grim sense of responsibility settling over him. Mnemosyne, he now realizes, is not just a single project confined to one lab or one scientist. It represents an entire frontier of research, and those with the resources and ambition to pursue it will continue, no matter the obstacles.

He quickly contacts Mr. Murthy, who has remained vigilant and loyal in monitoring Mnemosyne's security. They meet under the cover of night at a remote location, where Suborno shares his findings and the implications of the USB drive. Murthy's face turns pale as he listens, the realization dawning that this struggle is far from over.

"We may have stopped Venkatesh, but this is only a glimpse of the larger picture," Murthy says solemnly. "There are forces some of which we probably don't even know about who want this technology at any cost."

They both understand what must be done. This threat is too great for any one individual or organization to handle. It requires a coordinated, global effort a coalition of minds and forces, each bringing their unique strengths to secure Mnemosyne's secrets from those who would misuse them.

In the following weeks, Suborno and Murthy begin reaching out to trusted allies worldwide. They form a discreet network of intelligence officials, cyber-security experts, ethical scientists, and international law enforcers. This "Mnemosyne Consortium," as they call it, is dedicated to monitoring, intercepting, and dismantling any attempt to replicate or weaponize memory manipulation technology. Its members operate in secret, bound by a shared oath to protect humanity from the dangers of altered minds and artificial memories.

The Consortium establishes protocols for tracking suspicious activity across scientific, technological, and intelligence communities. They develop a secure communication system, hidden behind layers of encrypted servers, to share updates on potential threats. Each member is given specific roles, from surveillance and intelligence gathering to crisis management and diplomatic liaison.

Chapter Twenty Three - Breakthrough

Months later, Suborno learns of a breakthrough within the Consortium, a promising new technology that can detect artificial memory implants in an individual's brain. This tool, while in its infancy, gives them an edge, enabling them to identify cases where Mnemosyne-like techniques have been applied. It allows the Consortium to expose unethical research practices, shut down illegal experiments, and raise public awareness of the dangers of memory manipulation.

Despite the Consortium's efforts, whispers of Mnemosyne continue to surface. A few rogue scientists vanish under mysterious circumstances, laboratories are raided by unknown assailants, and encrypted files circulate on the dark web, hinting at breakthroughs in memory technology. Suborno realizes that the battle over Mnemosyne is becoming a global cat-and-mouse game, with no end in sight.

Meanwhile, rumors spread of a mysterious figure known only as "The Shadow." Some say he is a former intelligence officer with a vendetta, others believe he is a tech genius obsessed with immortality, and a few think he might even be a victim of Mnemosyne himself, struggling with fractured memories. Whoever he is, The Shadow emerges as a dangerous player, willing to fund any experiment, bribe any official, and manipulate anyone necessary to get closer to the ultimate goal: full mastery over human memory.

Suborno realizes that The Shadow may be the embodiment of the darker side of Mnemosyne; a reminder of the lengths people will go to control others. The Consortium begins focusing on this elusive figure, hoping to intercept him before he can cause irreparable damage.

In the story's final chapters, the stage is set for a dramatic clash. The Consortium stands united, prepared to protect the future by keeping Mnemosyne out of the wrong hands. Suborno is once again at the center, his mind sharp, his instincts honed, and his determination unshakable. Yet, even he understands that this is only the beginning of a long, uncertain journey.

As he prepares for the challenges ahead, Suborno finds himself thinking of Dr. Kapoor is now living peacefully and oblivious to the storm around him. In that moment, Suborno knows his purpose: to safeguard the knowledge that Dr. Kapoor left behind, not just for his friend's sake, but for the world.

As Dr. Kapoor's book ends, readers are left with a tantalizing hint: a coded message arrives for Suborno, bearing the signature of The Shadow. "See you in the field, Detective," it reads, a subtle promise of a confrontation that will test every limit, moral and mental, in the struggle for control over human memory.

The readers are left on the edge, awaiting the next book, where Suborno and the Consortium will take their fight against The Shadow to the global stage, racing against time to protect a technology that could either elevate or enslave humanity. And as Suborno steels himself for the unknown, he knows that the journey to secure Mnemosyne has only just begun.

In a dimly lit laboratory deep within the fortified research complex, a team of scientists and neurologists gathered around a single surgical bed, their eyes focused on the still figure lying upon it. This wasn't just another experiment. They were on the cusp of a groundbreaking procedure that, if successful, could redefine the boundaries of life, memory, and human capability.

The subject on the table was a middle-aged man who had lived a quiet, unremarkable life as an office clerk. For most of his years, he'd led a routine existence, displaying none of the remarkable creativity or talent that would leave a lasting legacy. But, today, he was about to receive a fragment of genius; the part of the brain from one of India's most celebrated musicians, who had tragically lost his life in a car accident only ten hours earlier.

This wasn't the first experiment in brain transplant research. The scientists in Dr. Kapoor's team had perfected transplants from brain to brain, testing on cadavers and conducting countless simulations. But this time, they were venturing into uncharted territory transplanting not just tissue but talent, creativity, and perhaps even the remnants of a lifetime's memories and emotions, into the living mind of someone who had never experienced them.

Dr. Kapoor himself, observing from behind a secure glass partition, felt a mixture of excitement and apprehension. He knew the risks involved. The brain, after all, was not a simple organ; it held the essence of what made each person unique; their memories, talents, dreams, and even their deepest fears. And in this case, they were transplanting a piece of the cerebral cortex, responsible for creativity, memory, and musical perception.

As the procedure began, the lab was eerily quiet, with only the rhythmic beeps of the monitoring machines filling the air. The team worked with meticulous precision, isolating the part of the musician's brain they had preserved and gently inserting it into the prepared cavity in the subject's brain. Every movement was cautious, controlled, each step carefully planned and executed as they integrated the musician's brain tissue into the man's own neural network.

Hours passed, and the procedure came to an end. The subject lay motionless as the scientists waited, holding their collective breaths, watching the EEG readings for any sign of neural activity. Minutes passed without any response, and some of the younger researchers exchanged nervous glances, fearing the experiment had failed. Then, almost imperceptibly, a faint spark appeared on the monitor a sign of brain activity.

The subject's eyes fluttered open, and he stared at the ceiling in confusion. Dr. Kapoor entered the room and leaned over him, speaking in a calm, measured tone. "How are you feeling?"

The man blinked, his eyes darting around the room as if seeing everything for the first time. He looked down at his hands, turning them over, a faint frown creasing his forehead. Then, in a voice that was barely more than a whisper, he said, "I hear...music."

The scientists looked at one another in shock. The man had never shown any particular interest or aptitude for music before. He had no training, no experience. And yet, here he was, describing a sensation that could only come from the memories and abilities of the late musician.

Intrigued Dr. Kapoor leaned closer, observing the man with a penetrating gaze. "What do you mean music? Can you describe it?"

The man's eyes unfocused slightly, as he spoke; as if he was recalling a distant memory. "It's...a melody. It's beautiful, like...something I've heard before but can't quite place." His fingers twitched involuntarily, tapping out an invisible rhythm, a gesture eerily reminiscent of the musician himself.

Dr. Kapoor motioned for a researcher to bring a tablet, and with a few taps, he pulled up a simple music composition app. He handed it to the man, who took it with a strange familiarity. Slowly, hesitantly, he began tapping on the screen, creating a soft, haunting melody that filled the lab with its delicate notes. The scientists watched in astonishment; the melody was unmistakably similar to one of the compositions by the deceased musician.

Over the next few days, the man's progress was nothing short of astounding. He began displaying not only musical talent but also intricate knowledge of scales, rhythms, and compositions. He spoke of musical techniques he couldn't possibly have learned on his own, recalling compositions and improvising in ways that matched the late musician's style.

It was a breakthrough, a seemingly miraculous transformation that suggested that not only skills but even fragments of personality could be transferred through a brain transplant. But the success was shadowed by unexpected complications.

At night, the man would wake in a panic, haunted by dreams of the musician's past—places he had never visited, people he had never met. He described flashes of memories: being on stage, hearing applause, feeling the rush of performance, and even the terror of the accident. It was as if the musician's mind had left imprints that were now struggling to reconcile themselves within a new host.

Chapter Twenty Four - Semi-Incarnation

The psychological toll was immense. The man began questioning his own identity, unsure whether he was himself or a reincarnation of the musician's mind. He would look at his reflection in the mirror, confused, sometimes talking to himself as though he were two people trapped in a single body.

Recognizing the risk, Dr. Kapoor's team stepped in providing therapy to help the man differentiate between his own memories and the ones he had acquired. They guided him through meditation and mental exercises, helping him accept the foreign memories without letting them consume his sense of self.

The breakthrough attracted global attention, though the nature of the experiment remained classified. Word spread among elite circles that Dr. Kapoor's laboratory had unlocked the secret to transferring not only skills but fragments of identity. Speculation grew that the technology, if refined, could be used to preserve the minds of great thinkers, artists, and scientists, granting humanity a way to immortalize its brightest minds and pass them onto future generations.

Yet Dr. Kapoor and his team knew the ethical implications of such a technology. Could a person's life experiences and talents truly be considered a transferable asset, or would they merely impose a fragmented identity upon another person? Would the original personality of the recipient eventually be overshadowed by the talents and memories of the donor? Could such a transplant ultimately erode the very essence of individual identity?

As the man's progress stabilized, a new sense of foreboding settled over Dr. Kapoor. He had opened a door to a world that could irrevocably alter the course of human identity and legacy. With further research, the potential to manipulate and transfer identities across bodies was becoming more feasible, but he questioned whether humanity was ready for such a leap.

Meanwhile, rumors began to circulate about shadowy groups who were desperate to get their hands on the brain transplant technology, seeing it as the key to controlling the future of human minds. It was no longer just a scientific achievement; it was a strategic asset, one with the power to redefine life, memory, and identity. As security tightened around the lab and the surrounding fortified complex Dr. Kapoor realized that the greatest challenge ahead would not be the science but ensuring that the knowledge remained in safe hands, protected from those who would wield it without restraint.

In the closing scenes of this phase, the man is seen playing the melody from the musician's memories once again, his expression one of both awe and confusion. It's as if he has accepted that he is now a blend of two lives, two minds sharing one body. Dr. Kapoor watches from a distance, feeling the weight of what they've achieved and the burden of responsibility it brings.

This moment marks the beginning of a new chapter in Dr. Kapoor's research, a chapter where the boundaries between life and memory, identity and talent, would be tested like never before. As he contemplates the next steps, he is haunted by the knowledge that others, too, are watching, waiting for the opportunity to seize this technology for their own purposes. The journey ahead is uncertain, fraught with ethical dilemmas and the looming presence of those who would stop at nothing to harness the power of memory manipulation, and as the fortified walls of the lab seem to close in, Dr. Kapoor prepares himself for the battles that lie ahead, knowing that the very future of human identity hangs in the balance.

As days passed, the implications of the experiment settled heavily on the team. Dr. Kapoor couldn't shake the feeling that they had crossed a threshold that science might never have been meant to approach. The man who now possessed the musician's memories and skills showed remarkable progress, but with it came a troubling intensity. He would lose himself in the music, eyes vacant, and fingers moving instinctively over instruments he had never played before the transplant. His own memories seemed distant, overshadowed by the musical genius now entangled with his mind.

Dr. Kapoor's concern grew each day as he observed this identity blending. He found himself questioning the long-term impact of these foreign memories on the man's sense of self. Would he permanently lose parts of his original identity, consumed by the borrowed talent and fragments of another person's life?

Meanwhile, word of the experiment's success spread through clandestine channels. Powerful individuals and private organizations, intrigued by the possibility of "memory transference," began contacting those close to Dr. Kapoor's inner circle. Offers came in from shadowy entities—some claiming to be from defense sectors, others from private interests with vast resources. Each approached with promises of funding and power, hoping to gain control over the lab and its groundbreaking technology.

Recognizing the growing danger, Dr. Kapoor took precautionary steps to strengthen the lab's defenses. Additional security protocols were implemented, and access to certain sections of the facility became heavily restricted. Even the local staff working in the agricultural land surrounding the lab, were kept under closer observation. Dr. Kapoor knew that such measures could only offer limited protection. Once word had spread, it was only a matter of time before someone with serious power would try to seize control.

The first sign of this came in the form of an anonymous message delivered through encrypted channels. The message read:

"The age of human limitations is over. You hold the key to unlocking our true potential. We will come for it soon."

Dr. Kapoor, who had spent decades pushing the boundaries of science, felt an unexpected chill as he read the words. He realized that this breakthrough, if it fell into the wrong hands, could be turned into a weapon; a way to control not just minds but also hearts, motivations, and ultimately, identities.

Despite the growing tension Dr. Kapoor and his team continued to refine their research in secret. They began conducting experiments to understand the process more deeply, attempting to uncover ways to limit the psychological and emotional bleed-through that was occurring. However, they soon discovered a troubling phenomenon: the memory fragments were not only blending but, in some cases, appearing to "adapt" within the host brain, suggesting that there might be more to memories than mere neural connections. It raised questions about whether memory could carry traces of personality and consciousness beyond simple skills and knowledge.

One night, a breakthrough of a different kind occurred. A strange incident brought new urgency to their research. The man with the musician's memories was seen wandering the laboratory complex late at night, muttering to himself and playing an invisible piano. When the security guards approached him, he looked up with an expression that was both dazed and terrified.

"I'm... I'm not me," he whispered, his voice trembling. "I feel as if I'm living in someone else's dreams."

Dr. Kapoor realized that the identity crisis was worsening. The original memories and personality of the musician seemed to be resurfacing within the man's mind, as if trying to assert control. It was no longer just about memory transference; it was as if a fragment of the musician's essence was struggling to manifest within the host. The man's words echoed in Dr. Kapoor's mind: Was it possible for memories to contain pieces of consciousness?

As Dr. Kapoor delved deeper into these implications, a new, pressing crisis emerged. The intelligence agencies had picked up chatter of foreign interest in the lab's research. High-ranking officials warned Dr. Kapoor that agents might already be attempting to infiltrate the complex. In response, they escalated security to unprecedented levels, going as far as to implement counter-surveillance teams within the lab and the surrounding village to detect any suspicious activity.

Then, a chilling event transpired. A scientist, who worked closely with Dr. Kapoor, vanished without a trace. The disappearance shook the entire team, particularly when they learned that the missing scientist was last seen carrying sensitive documents related to the memory transfer experiments. Fearing an internal leak, Dr. Kapoor's team conducted a thorough sweep of the facility, but no further clues were found.

They intensified their investigation; Dr. Kapoor received a visit from an unlikely source: a senior intelligence official who had been closely monitoring the case. The official, a stern, calculating man, had been informed of Dr. Kapoor's work and now demanded answers.

"We are aware of the potential of this technology," the official said, his tone cold. "But you must understand, Doctor, that what you have created here could destabilize the very fabric of society. We cannot allow it to fall into the wrong hands. You must consider surrendering your research to government oversight."

Dr. Kapoor hesitated, feeling a conflict between the need for security and his dedication to scientific freedom. Handing over the research could mean losing control of the technology, potentially weaponizing it. Yet refusing might invite more dangerous players to take matters into their own hands.

After a tense silence Dr. Kapoor spoke carefully. "I understand your concern. But I need you to realize that this technology isn't simply a tool; it's a double-edged sword. Without the proper understanding, it could destroy lives just as easily as it could enhance them."

The official's expression softened slightly, though his eyes remained steely. "Then let us work together,

Doctor. But be warned: if we detect any attempt to compromise national security, we will intervene directly."

With that, the official left, and Dr. Kapoor was left with a difficult decision. He knew that if he agreed to work closely with the government, he could potentially secure protection and resources. Yet, he feared that even they might misuse the technology, given its incredible power. But the threats to his lab, his team, and even his own life had reached a point where he could no longer ignore them.

After much contemplation Dr. Kapoor devised a plan. He would agree to partial cooperation with the intelligence agency, providing controlled access to his research while keeping the most critical aspects under strict security. He would compartmentalize the information, sharing only what was essential, while safeguarding the full scope of his work. Additionally, he began creating a detailed journal, documenting the ethical dilemmas and potential consequences of his research, hoping that if something were to happen to him, his concerns would live on.

Over the next few months, Dr. Kapoor and his team worked under intense scrutiny. Security protocols were increased, and every member of the lab was closely monitored. The tension was palpable as the line between scientific discovery and military interest blurred.

Chapter Twenty Five - Breach and Treachery

Then, one day, Dr. Kapoor's worst fears came true. A coded message arrived on his secure terminal, relaying a breach attempt on the lab's outer defenses. An unknown group, heavily armed, was moving toward the complex, attempting to bypass the seven layers of security. It was unclear whether they were foreign agents or a rogue faction interested in the technology, but their intent was unmistakable.

With minutes to react, Dr. Kapoor activated the lab's highest security protocol. He led his team into a concealed bunker within the facility and ensured that the most critical data was encrypted and stored on a remote server that could only be accessed with a special key.

As the security alarms blared, Dr. Kapoor glanced around at his team, feeling both the weight of responsibility and the resolve to protect his work. This was no longer just about scientific discovery. It was a battle to safeguard the future of human identity and memory itself.

The intruders were intercepted by security forces before they could reach the inner chambers of the lab. But the incident served as a stark reminder: the world had changed, and so had the stakes. Dr. Kapoor understood that his research would forever remain a target, and that his work would have consequences he couldn't yet foresee.

As he stood in the silent lab surrounded by the equipment and computer screens that had once represented the promise of human advancement, he felt a strange sense of foreboding. He knew that this was only the beginning of a much larger struggle, one that would force him to make unimaginable choices. And as the echoes of footsteps faded in the corridors outside, he wondered whether humanity was ready for the power he had unlocked, or if, like Pandora's Box, it would unleash a force that could never be contained again.

The days following the breach attempt left Dr. Kapoor and his team on edge. Although the intruders had been stopped, their intent was clear: they would return, and next time, they might be better prepared. Dr. Kapoor decided it was time to shift the lab's research underground, in every sense of the word.

First, he coordinated with his trusted colleagues to create multiple layers of fail-safes. If their work was ever compromised, the most crucial research files would be instantly erased, and all experimental data would be fragmented and scattered across secure servers around the world. Dr. Kapoor also moved part of the memory transfer equipment into hidden compartments within the lab, accessible only through biometric and multi-factor authentication known solely to him and a few loyal associates.

Under this intensified security, he refocused his team on refining their understanding of memory and identity integration, hoping to better control the psychological effects of memory transfers. They began conducting experiments on small, non-invasive memory implants, trying to understand which parts of memory could be safely transferred without overwhelming the recipient's consciousness. The goal was no longer to enable full memory transfers but to build a sustainable framework for limited memory transplants, minimizing risks to the recipient's identity.

Despite his efforts to keep everything contained, Dr. Kapoor noticed an increasing paranoia among his team. Every unexplained sound, every unexpected visitor to the facility was seen as a potential threat. And then, on an otherwise calm evening, one of his senior researchers approached him with urgent news.

"Dr. Kapoor, I have reason to believe there's a mole within our team," the researcher said, her voice barely a whisper. "There are strange signals being transmitted from our internal network. I traced them, but they keep vanishing and reappearing, as if someone is trying to cover their tracks."

The revelation was a blow. Dr. Kapoor had handpicked each team member, believing them to be trustworthy and committed. But the thought of a betrayal from within meant that the breach attempts might not have been random or isolated events. Someone with insider knowledge was feeding information to outside parties, and that realization sent a chill down his spine.

Deciding to act swiftly Dr. Kapoor instructed the researcher to conduct a secretive investigation into all communications originating from within the facility. Each network signal, every email, and all file transfers would be scrutinized for irregularities. Meanwhile, he held a meeting with the team to re-emphasize the importance of their mission's secrecy, careful not to reveal his suspicions.

The days that followed were tense, with everyone on high alert. Then, one night, Dr. Kapoor was working late in his lab when the researcher knocked on his door, her face pale and eyes wide with shock.

"Dr. Kapoor," she whispered, "I've found the mole."

She handed him a set of encrypted files she'd intercepted from the lab's network. As Dr. Kapoor went through the data, his heart sank. The mole was one of his most trusted assistants, someone who had been with him from the beginning of the memory transfer experiments. The assistant had been leaking information, albeit in fragments, to a powerful private corporation with connections in multiple countries. This corporation was a front for a covert organization seeking to control memory transfer technology for its own hidden agendas.

Dr. Kapoor confronted the assistant the following morning, in the privacy of his office. The assistant, initially shocked, eventually broke down and confessed. He had been promised a fortune and assured that his family would be taken care of, if only he would help secure the research for the organization.

"Do you understand what you've done?" Dr. Kapoor said his voice a mix of anger and sadness. "This isn't just about money or career advancement. This technology has the potential to alter humanity itself, to redefine identity and consciousness. If it falls into the wrong hands, we could lose control of our own memories, our very selves."

But the assistant, defeated and ashamed, could only mutter, "I didn't think it would go this far."

Dr. Kapoor decided not to report the incident to the authorities just yet. Instead, he and the researcher orchestrated a plan to use the assistant's position to their advantage. They fed him controlled, fabricated information about their research, effectively turning him into an unknowing double agent. This allowed Dr. Kapoor to track the movements of the covert organization, giving him valuable insights into their plans.

Meanwhile, Dr. Kapoor also worked on creating an emergency communication channel with high-ranking government officials who had supported his research. He realized that any attempt to keep the technology entirely independent was futile. It was clear that he needed allies in the intelligence and defense sectors who shared his ethical concerns and who could help protect the project from commercial exploitation and militarization.

Dr. Kapoor's lab operated in an atmosphere of intense secrecy and layered deception. With every step forward in memory research, they disguised their true progress, creating the appearance of setbacks and failures in case outside forces were observing. They intentionally slowed down their official reports, ensuring that anyone watching from the shadows would underestimate the true capabilities of the technology.

However, the deception took a toll. Dr. Kapoor's team grew weary, burdened by the constant surveillance and pressure. Tensions among the team members increased, as trust eroded under the weight of suspicion. Some members left, unable to endure the strain, but Dr. Kapoor kept pushing forward, knowing that if they abandoned the research, the covert organization would surely pick up where they left off.

After some days, on a fateful moment Dr. Kapoor received an unexpected message on his encrypted line. It was a warning from his allies in the intelligence community. A sophisticated attempt was being planned to infiltrate the lab and seize control of the memory transfer technology. This time, it was more than just a reconnaissance mission; it was a full-scale operation involving some of the most dangerous covert operatives.

The warning gave Dr. Kapoor only a few hours to act. He activated the final phase of his contingency plan. He called his remaining team members together and explained the imminent danger.

"We can no longer keep this technology here. If they come for it, we may not be able to stop them," Dr. Kapoor said. "We're going to decentralize everything. Each of you will take a piece of our research, encrypted and concealed, and go to separate locations. We'll regroup once the threat has passed, but for now, we must protect our work and scatter."

In a coordinated effort, the team dismantled the lab's core systems, encrypting the data into fragments and dispersing it among themselves. They made plans to rendezvous at a secure location months later, once they were confident the threat had dissipated.

Dr. Kapoor watched his team disperse into the night he felt a pang of regret. This research, his life's work, was now a hunted treasure, and the idealistic dream of advancing human knowledge had turned into a shadowy battle for control. Yet, he was resolute. He would rather lose the technology than allow it to be corrupted and used for exploitation.

Before leaving the lab for the last time Dr. Kapoor looked around the facility that had been his sanctuary, the place where groundbreaking science had been born. He felt a sense of closure as he activated the lab's self-destruct mechanism, erasing any trace of the technology.

The lab faded into darkness. Dr. Kapoor knew that the struggle was far from over. The organization would continue its pursuit, and one day, he and his team would have to face them again. But for now, they had bought themselves precious time.

And in that time Dr. Kapoor would prepare, strategize, and seek new allies. This was no longer just a scientific endeavor; it was a quest for survival, a battle to protect humanity's right to retain its true self.

Dr. Kapoor drove away from the lab, the silhouette of the mountains rising against the dawn he couldn't help but feel that this was only the beginning. The stakes were higher than ever, and the world had yet to realize the power that memory held the very essence of human identity, and a force that would either unify or divide humanity like never before.

The dust settled after Dr. Kapoor and his team's last-ditch effort to protect their research, another storm was quietly brewing. Three assistant directors had recently arrived at the Chinese Embassy in New Delhi under the guise of diplomatic appointments. However, these operatives had a much darker mission: they were here to extract two Chinese agents imprisoned on sedation and abduction charges, agents directly tied to the earlier attempts to infiltrate Dr. Kapoor's lab. This operation, known as "Phoenix Protocol" among the assistant directors, was a carefully planned rescue mission aimed at retrieving not just the agents but also vital intelligence on Dr. Kapoor's research work.

The assistant directors quickly established contact with a few disillusioned police officers within the Indian ranks officers who felt overlooked or frustrated in their roles. Promising them considerable wealth and a fast-track escape plan, the Chinese agents skillfully planted a seed of discontent, convincing the officers to collude in their mission.

One quiet evening, under the cover of darkness, the three Chinese operatives, accompanied by the compromised officers executed their plan. The Indian police had been informed that a minor electrical issue was detected in the security block where the two Chinese agents were being held, providing a perfect excuse to create a small-scale distraction. As the officers pretended to check the wiring in the area, the agents managed to slip the prisoners out of their cells.

The prison break was smooth, almost too easy. Within minutes, the two agents and their rescuers were out of the compound, slipping through a hidden exit that led to a series of back alleys. A convoy of inconspicuous vehicles waited outside, their engines already running. The plan was to drive to the coast, where a cargo ship would transport them to a port in Southeast Asia, beyond the reach of Indian law enforcement.

But just as the convoy started to move, alarms blared throughout the prison, triggered by an alert guard who noticed suspicious activity on the surveillance feeds. Within moments, the police station was alive with flashing lights and panicked radio calls. The alarm was quickly relayed to higher authorities, and within minutes, a full-scale manhunt was underway.

The Chinese convoy raced through the city streets, weaving through traffic at breakneck speed. Indian police, now mobilized with everything from patrol cars to unmarked SUVs, pursued relentlessly. The chase took them through narrow lanes, crowded markets, and highways, each turn more harrowing than the last. Knowing they needed to throw the pursuers off, the Chinese operatives had planned to switch vehicles in a secluded location by the docks.

When they reached the dockside hideout, the group quickly swapped their vehicles for an unmarked cargo truck already arranged by their contacts. Loading into the truck, they sped towards the coast, where a ship awaited their arrival. They believed they had outmaneuvered the authorities, but unknown to them, the Indian intelligence agency had already intercepted their communications with the ship. Indian coast guards were now ready and waiting.

When the truck finally reached the coast and pulled up beside the ship, a group of men dressed as dock workers quietly moved into position. As the Chinese agents disembarked from the truck, two of the "dock workers" sprang into action, blocking the gangway. Suddenly, police spotlights illuminated the entire area, and a booming voice shouted over a loudspeaker, demanding the agents surrender.

Panicking, the group split up, with some heading back to the truck and others trying to board the ship. A firefight broke out as the agents desperately tried to escape, using the crates and barrels on the dock for cover. In the chaos, a few managed to slip aboard a smaller boat docked nearby. They sped off into the open sea, hoping to evade capture and reach international waters.

However, the Indian authorities were ready for this contingency. A patrol boat was immediately dispatched, and a high-speed chase ensued across the choppy waters. The agents, realizing they had no escape, finally attempted a desperate radio call to a contact stationed at a nearby private airstrip.

The remaining agents managed to reach the airstrip and hijack a small, private plane. They took off under cover of night, hoping to make it out of Indian airspace. Yet again, the Indian authorities anticipated their move and scrambled fighter jets to intercept the aircraft. The jets flanked the plane, ordering it to land or face dire consequences.

Surrounded and outmatched, the hijacked plane was forced to touch down at a nearby airbase. As it landed, police and military personnel swarmed the aircraft, detaining everyone on board. The three assistant directors from the Chinese Embassy, the two escaped agents, three corrupt Indian officers, and a previously unknown Chinese intelligence operative posing as a cargo ship captain were taken into custody.

In the interrogation rooms, the suspects initially stayed silent, hoping for diplomatic immunity. But with mounting evidence, and facing the unyielding pressure from Indian interrogators, cracks began to appear in their facade. Eventually, one of the assistant directors broke, revealing the reason behind their mission. The agents admitted that the Chinese government had a vested interest in obtaining Dr. Kapoor's brain transplant technology, specifically for military applications. They saw potential in enhancing soldier performance, creating agents with perfect memory recall, and even transferring strategic knowledge across individuals, effectively immortalizing elite operatives.

One assistant director explained further, "Imagine a soldier with the expertise of a hundred veterans, or an intelligence operative who can absorb the memories of every agent who came before them. The applications are endless and the power, unimaginable."

The confession stunned the Indian authorities. This revelation transformed the case from an isolated incident of industrial espionage to a serious national security threat. The potential misuse of memory transfer technology in warfare posed ethical and humanitarian dangers that were hard to ignore.

In response, the Indian government imposed new security measures around Dr. Kapoor's research project. Layers of intelligence operatives were positioned in and around his facility, creating a protective web that even the most resourceful agents would find impossible to penetrate. Only the most trusted personnel were allowed access to the core research, and any foreign diplomat's movement was scrutinized to prevent further infiltration attempts.

This incident ignited international tensions, sparking concern among global powers. Dr. Kapoor was now operating in a high-stakes environment, with the knowledge that every discovery he made could reshape global security dynamics. But despite the political turmoil, he remained focused on the ethical implications of his research. He vowed to ensure that his life's work would serve humanity, not enable its destruction.

For the first time in years Dr. Kapoor felt a renewed sense of purpose; not merely as a scientist but as a custodian of knowledge that, in the wrong hands, could change the very fabric of society. And as he prepared for the challenges ahead, he couldn't help but wonder about the shadowy forces that would stop at nothing to claim his technology.

The world had become a different place, and Dr. Kapoor was now at the heart of a conflict that extended beyond national borders and scientific inquiry.

Suborno Deb Barman sat silently, piecing together the final fragments of this dark and twisted puzzle. The moment had come to recover the stolen brain of Dr. Venkatraman, and his instincts told him the thieves would attempt an escape soon. With the facility's security compromised, the chances of fleeing undetected through traditional means were slim. Suborno's hunch pointed towards Nepal a transit hub where the international criminal network could operate with ease, given its challenging borders and frequent private flights.

Within hours, Suborno coordinated with Inspector Karthik Singh, creating a plan to intercept the perpetrators. They would conduct a sting operation, placing undercover agents at each step to monitor the situation without alarming the suspects. This final operation required Suborno's most meticulous planning; any misstep could lead the criminals to destroy the brain rather than risk its recovery.

Chapter Twenty Six - The Setup: Preparing the Net

Suborno divided his team into several groups. The plan was to set up checkpoints in multiple stages, forcing the suspects to follow a carefully orchestrated path that would lead them right into the net. Singh's team, disguised as tourists positioned themselves in the arrival lounge of Kathmandu's Tribhuvan International Airport; a second team disguised as airport staff stationed themselves near check-in counters and exits. Suborno himself would wait at a safe distance, ready to act on the slightest sign of movement.

Meanwhile, a hidden surveillance van parked near the airport's entrance would feed live footage of the lounge area. Using this mobile control room, Suborno could communicate with each team, coordinate actions, and ensure that no one made a move until he gave the signal. Time was crucial; intelligence reports indicated the suspects would arrive by late afternoon.

To avoid raising suspicion, the undercover agents blended in seamlessly with the crowd. Some posed as local businessmen, while others mingled with tourists, ensuring that any potential suspects would feel comfortable before making a move. Every member of

Suborno's team understood the importance of patience in this delicate operation.

The Arrival: A Game of Cat and Mouse

As the clock neared 4 p.m., a man in his mid-thirties entered the lounge, casually dressed in jeans and a leather jacket. His eyes scanned the surroundings with an intensity that suggested more than mere curiosity. Suborno quickly recognized him from surveillance footage: one of the thieves involved in the theft at the lab. Moments later, another suspect, a tall woman with short hair, arrived. She glanced at her wristwatch before nodding subtly at the man. Their movements were methodical, careful. Suborno's instinct told him these two were professionals.

Through a discreet earpiece, Suborno directed his team to observe but maintain distance. They would let the suspects settle, waiting for the third thief to arrive. As expected, within minutes, a third person joined them; a man with a large duffel bag slung over his shoulder. Suborno knew the brain was likely in that bag, concealed in specialized medical equipment to keep it viable.

The three thieves exchanged a few words before moving toward a secluded area in the lounge. Suborno's team followed at a distance, strategically positioning them at every possible exit. Suborno observed carefully, waiting for the right moment to make his move.

The Distraction: Sowing Confusion

To execute the arrest smoothly, Suborno planned a distraction. Two officers, disguised as quarrelsome tourists, approached the suspects, accidentally bumping into the man with the duffel bag. An argument ensued, and the suspect's irritation grew as he attempted to avoid unwanted attention. This minor altercation provided Suborno's team with a crucial advantage: it gave them the chance to get closer without raising suspicion.

At that moment, Suborno, dressed as an airport maintenance worker, subtly approached the lounge area. He knew the suspects were on edge; the altercation had unsettled them, making them more likely to act impulsively. His plan was working; each small disruption increased their anxiety, pushing them closer to a mistake.

The Chase: Unmasking the Suspects

Suddenly, the man with the duffel bag seemed to realize he was under surveillance. Without warning, he bolted toward the nearest exit, followed by his accomplices. Suborno sprang into action, signaling his team to pursue them. The lounge erupted in chaos as the suspects sprinted through the terminal, dodging passengers and airport staff.

Singh and another officer chased them through the crowded corridors, weaving past bewildered travelers and airport personnel. The suspects reached an emergency stairwell, descending rapidly toward a side entrance that led to the airport's exterior. But as they exited, they were met with a barrier: more officers in position, blocking every possible escape route.

Realizing they were cornered, the suspects split up, each heading in a different direction. Suborno directed his team to divide and conquer, assigning pairs to pursue each suspect. He personally followed the man with the duffel bag, determined to secure the brain at all costs.

A High-Stakes Confrontation: The Streets of Kathmandu

The man with the duffel bag ran through the bustling streets of Kathmandu, dodging vendors and pedestrians in a desperate attempt to shake off his pursuers. Suborno, however, remained relentless, his focus unbroken as he followed the thief through narrow alleys and winding paths. Singh and another officer trailed close behind, coordinating with Suborno to corner the man.

Just as the suspect attempted to cross a narrow bridge, Suborno signaled to Singh to cut him off from the other side. Trapped, the man pulled out a small weapon, waving it defensively as he clutched the duffel bag. But Suborno knew he had to act decisively the precious cargo could not be allowed to fall into enemy hands.

With a swift maneuver, Suborno disarmed the man, sending the weapon skidding across the ground. A tense struggle ensued, the thief desperately holding onto the duffel bag, but Suborno's determination proved stronger. Finally, with a decisive grip, he tore the bag from the suspect's grasp and handed it to Singh, who secured it carefully. The thief, exhausted and defeated, sank to the ground.

Meanwhile, the rest of the team had successfully apprehended the other two suspects. All three were taken into custody, each under tight security to prevent any chance of escape.

The Interrogation: The Truth Uncovered

Back in New Delhi, Suborno and Singh prepared for the final phase of their mission. The suspects were interrogated in a secure facility, where they gradually revealed the extent of their intentions. Under rigorous questioning, the thieves confessed to their orders from a covert faction within a foreign government. Their objective had been to use Dr. Venkatraman's preserved brain to replicate his intellect within their own military.

As the interrogation progressed, more chilling details emerged. This group was developing an entire program based on transferring the skills and genius of deceased experts into select operatives. If successful, it would have given them access to knowledge and insights beyond their own capabilities, creating an elite force powered by the world's greatest minds.

The Resolution: Securing the Brain

Suborno knew that retrieving the brain was only part of his mission. Ensuring its safe return and preventing any future attempts to weaponize such technology became his priority. After the suspects were detained, the brain was transported under heavy guard to a top-secret government lab. Specialists carefully examined it to confirm its integrity, and further security measures were implemented to prevent any future breaches.

When the brain was finally returned to Dr. Venkatraman's family, it came with strict orders for its preservation under government oversight. The family expressed both relief and gratitude, deeply moved by the efforts to recover it.

The Hidden War

With the mission complete, Suborno reflected on the gravity of what had transpired. He knew this was no ordinary case; it was a glimpse into a future where human potential could be exploited, where the boundaries of life and death blurred under the guise of scientific progress. This was only the beginning, he sensed, of a hidden war over technology that could change the course of history.

As he left the facility, he couldn't shake the feeling that this case would haunt him. The files were closed, the suspects in custody, but somewhere, in the shadows, forces were already regrouping, seeking the next breakthrough.

Suborno understood that his work was far from over.

In the quiet aftermath of the case, Suborno returned to his office with an eerie sense that the mission's success had only scratched the surface of a much larger and more insidious network. Though the brain of Dr. Venkatraman had been recovered and safeguarded, the implications of the case lingered like a storm on the horizon. He knew that this was a glimpse into a new, high-stakes frontier—one that blended espionage with the dark edges of bioengineering and artificial intelligence.

A few days later, as he settled back into his routine, Suborno received an encrypted message on his secure device. The message contained a single line: "They're watching from the other side." Alongside it was an image of an unknown facility, a sterile and dimly lit room filled with strange medical apparatus and containment chambers. Although the photo had no obvious identifiers, his instincts told him this place was not in India. It felt like a direct challenge; a signal that the game was far from over.

Suborno studied the image carefully, noting the unnatural glow of the machinery, the indistinct figures shrouded in hazmat suits, and the faint outline of containment tanks that looked eerily similar to those used in cutting-edge neuroscience labs. He couldn't shake the feeling that this was connected to the Chinese operatives they had apprehended. Had the faction behind them already established other facilities? Was this their warning of what lay ahead?

Determined to find answers, Suborno started a fresh line of investigation. He reached out to his trusted allies in intelligence, planting inquiries that would ripple discreetly across various agencies without raising too much attention. He reviewed the interrogation tapes of the detained spies and cross-referenced every detail, hoping to find any overlooked clue or hint of the larger network. After days of searching, he found one obscure reference that stood out a name, seemingly insignificant, mentioned in passing by one of the operatives during his confession: "Project Phoenix."

Intrigued, Suborno expanded his research. "Project Phoenix" yielded scant results, and what little he found was buried deep within intelligence reports, coded in fragments. The project appeared to focus on transferring skills and intellectual prowess from one individual to another, a process far more complex than a simple memory transfer. This program aimed to harness the knowledge and instincts of exceptional individuals, military strategists, scientists, musicians, and thinkers—who were deceased or nearing the end of their lives. Their skills would be effectively resurrected within operatives who could then execute missions with unparalleled expertise.

Realizing the scope of the project, Suborno was both fascinated and horrified. The project's potential to reshape global power dynamics was undeniable. Imagine soldiers who fought with the tactical genius of history's greatest generals, or scientists who continued to innovate long after their deaths. The ethical and security implications were staggering, and if Project Phoenix was being pursued in secret facilities abroad, it could signify a new arms race, one fought with minds instead of weapons.

Suborno convened a meeting with his closest associates to discuss the next steps. Inspector Karthik

Singh, who had been a steadfast partner throughout the previous case, was visibly unsettled as Suborno laid out the details of Project Phoenix.

"This isn't just about intellectual theft anymore," Singh remarked gravely. "If this technology is perfected, it could redefine warfare. We'd be dealing with armies of super-soldiers, scientists, or strategists who are effectively immortal."

"We're dealing with something beyond warfare," Suborno responded. "We're looking at a world where identity, intelligence, and individuality could be commodified and controlled. Project Phoenix would allow the highest bidders to resurrect minds of unparalleled genius. It's a resurrection of expertise but a death of humanity."

Singh nodded, understanding the urgency of their task. They needed to disrupt the global operations of Project Phoenix before it grew too large to contain.

The Final Operation: Unmasking Project Phoenix

Working in the shadows, Suborno's team began coordinating with international partners. They gathered intelligence from various sources, confirming that Project Phoenix had covert installations not only in China but potentially in several other countries with vested interests in militarizing intelligence.

A breakthrough came when an anonymous informant, claiming to be a defected scientist from Project Phoenix, reached out to Suborno. The informant agreed to meet in a secure location, warning them that

Project Phoenix had already made significant advancements. They had successfully created what they called "Legacy Hosts" individuals implanted with the cognitive frameworks of deceased experts

Suborno and Singh organized a covert extraction mission to meet the informant in a neutral location, choosing a discreet safe house on the outskirts of Hong Kong. The informant arrived under heavy disguise, revealing chilling details about Project Phoenix's latest developments. According to the informant, the program's masterminds were now focusing on creating "Composite Hosts" individuals capable of housing multiple cognitive frameworks, thereby embodying the skills and strategies of numerous experts.

The informant handed over a list of coordinates for Phoenix facilities worldwide, marking each site with its function within the broader network. Suborno understood that he now possessed the key to dismantling Project Phoenix. But the informant's final words struck him with a new dread.

"They have begun targeting minds beyond the grave," the informant warned. "They are planning to extract the cognitive blueprints of historical figures. Imagine soldiers with the battlefield instincts of Alexander the Great or scientists with the inventive prowess of Nikola Tesla. That is their endgame."

With this disturbing revelation, Suborno knew that taking down Project Phoenix wasn't just a matter of intelligence anymore; it was a race to preserve the boundaries of human identity and autonomy. The implications went beyond military power; they threatened to rewrite history and reshape humanity's future.

The Take-Down: A Coordinated Global Strike

In the days that followed, Suborno and his international allies devised a multi-nation strategy to shut down Project Phoenix. Under the radar, intelligence agencies and Special Forces teams launched synchronized raids on Phoenix facilities worldwide. From labs hidden in industrial zones to secret installations in remote areas, Project Phoenix's operations were dismantled in a coordinated strike.

The final target was the central hub of Project Phoenix, located deep within a fortified compound in the mountainous region of Sichuan. Suborno joined an elite team tasked with breaching the compound. In a high-stakes operation, they navigated through sophisticated security systems and faced intense resistance from Phoenix operatives trained specifically to protect the project.

Inside, they uncovered the central archive a vault containing the encoded neural imprints of countless deceased experts, each representing a stolen legacy. With precise strikes, they dismantled the servers and disabled the machines that housed these imprints, effectively rendering Project Phoenix's most critical data inaccessible.

Epilogue: Restoring Balance

Back in India, Suborno took a quiet moment to reflect on the journey. He had seen the darkest corners of human ambition, where technology, ethics, and power intersected in a dangerous blend. Project Phoenix was averted, but the implications of this case would linger, a reminder of humanity's complex relationship with progress.

As he closed the final report on Project Phoenix, Suborno knew this wouldn't be the last time he would face the shadowy intersections of science and control. But for now, he had restored a fragile balance, protecting human identity from a future where it could be stripped, stolen, and exploited.

The case had ended, but its echoes would continue to shape Suborno's next pursuits. The world had seen only a fraction of the threats lying in wait, and he would be there, ready, vigilant, anticipating the next wave that would challenge the very fabric of humanity.

The aftermath of the Project Phoenix case brought both victories and tensions. In a retaliatory move, the Chinese government arrested three senior Indian officers in Beijing, heightening diplomatic strain. Indian authorities, however, negotiated a swift barter, exchanging the detained embassy officers. But two Chinese agents, along with the rogue healer, remained in Indian custody, now convicted of espionage and unethical experimentation.

Dr. Aryan Kapoor, a name etched in the annals of history, was a visionary who revolutionized the field of neurological engineering. Born into a humble family in a quaint village in India, his brilliance was evident from an early age. A curious mind and an insatiable thirst for knowledge led him to pursue the study of the human brain, the most enigmatic organ of the body. His groundbreaking contributions to memory locative research transformed our understanding of how memories are stored, retrieved, and even manipulated within the intricate networks of the brain.

Dr. Kapoor's journey was one of perseverance and passion. After completing his doctoral studies in neuroscience from a prestigious institute in India, he expanded his research globally. Collaborating with top minds across the world, he introduced innovative methods to map and stimulate neurological pathways. His revolutionary work laid the foundation for Neurological Engineering, a discipline that blends neuroscience, engineering, and computer science to create solutions for disorders like Alzheimer's, Parkinson's, and even memory loss due to trauma.

One of his most celebrated achievements was the development of the "Locative Memory Encoder" (LME), a device capable of aiding individuals in regaining lost memories. This innovation not only brought hope to millions suffering from neurological disorders but also inspired a new era of research in cognitive rehabilitation and enhancement. Governments, healthcare organizations, and scientific institutions hailed this breakthrough as a marvel of modern science.

For his unparalleled contributions, Dr. Kapoor was conferred with the prestigious Padma Bibhushan, India's second-highest civilian honor. The award ceremony was a moment of pride for the nation, with luminaries from across the world attending to pay homage to his genius. In his acceptance speech, Dr. Kapoor humbly dedicated the honor to his colleagues and the younger generation of researchers, urging them to continue unraveling the mysteries of the brain.

Despite his towering achievements, Dr. Kapoor remained a deeply grounded individual. His humility and dedication to humanity earned him love and respect far beyond the scientific community. He believed that science should serve society, often saying, "True success is measured by the number of lives you touch."

Great National Loss

Dr. Kapoor's demise due to age-related ailments was a monumental loss to the world. The entire scientific fraternity mourned his passing, with tributes pouring in from every corner of the globe. His absence created a void, but his legacy continues to inspire researchers, neurologists, and engineers worldwide. The Government of India, recognizing his invaluable contributions, declared his birthday as Neurological Day, a national observance to promote awareness and advancements in neurological sciences.

Today, Dr. Aryan Kapoor's name is synonymous with excellence in neuroscience. His pioneering spirit, relentless pursuit of knowledge, and commitment to bettering humanity remain an enduring inspiration. The world may have lost a great mind, but his work continues to light the path for generations to come.

The story of Dr. Kapoor reminds us that some individuals transcend the limitations of their time, leaving behind an everlasting legacy. And so, the world will never forget the man who unlocked the secrets of memory and gave hope to countless lives, Dr. Aryan Kapoor.

To honor Dr. Kapoor, a bronze statue was installed in the courtyard of his laboratory. At the unveiling ceremony, the Prime Minister personally acknowledged Dr. Kapoor's legacy, describing him as a visionary who had inspired India's scientific community. Under his shadow, India's researchers were now tasked with leading a new era of neurological advancement, bolstered by an unprecedented research grant to secure and elevate India's innovations.

As Suborno looked at the bronze statue gleaming under the morning sun, he felt a bittersweet pride. The case had brought closure, but it also opened the path for future breakthroughs and challenges in the field Dr. Kapoor had devoted his life to. The hunt was over, and India had secured a fragile victory in a game that stretched far beyond borders. Suborno knew that, while the mission had ended, the legacy of Dr. Kapoor would inspire a new generation of researchers who could keep this knowledge safe from prying eyes. All was well, for now, and Dr. Kapoor's spirit would live on in the minds of those who would dare to explore the frontiers he had unlocked.

P.S.

World would never know, how many time Dr. Kapoor went to retirement, how many times he destroyed his own laboratory and to what extent, and how many times he erased his own memory.

It was surely a blunder to launch his own book containing his pioneering neurological research.

About the Author

Aurobindo Ghosh

Dr. Aurobindo Ghosh, a distinguished scholar with an M.Sc., M.Phil., and dual Ph.D.s in Statistics and Economics, is a multifaceted individual—teacher, trainer, research guide, author, and artist.

His debut poetry collection, *Lily on the Northern Sky*, won an award from Ukiyoto Publishing and has been translated into French, German, Spanish, and Arabic. A regular contributor to Ukiyoto anthologies, his notable works include *Fairy and the Queen*, *Youngest Freedom Fighter Baji Raut*, *Make a Wish*, *Pinky Mehra Became Astronaut*, *Yudh Shastra*, *Nagoa Beach*, *Unity in Diversity: Unification of Germany*, *Mahakaal*, and *Upanishad*. *Unity in Diversity* is also available in German.

Dr. Ghosh's recent solo fiction, *Bimladadi's Dreams*, published by Ukiyoto, was recognized as the *Best Fiction Book of the Year* and adapted into an audiobook. It is now available in Italian, Turkish, and Nepali. Other solo works by him include *Mystical Honeymoon*, *Deception Redefined*, and *Chronicles of Detective Subroto Deb Barman*.

An accomplished artist, he creates acrylic, Warli, and Madhubani paintings. Writing in English, Bengali, Hindi,

Gujarati, and Marathi, Dr. Ghosh has also authored *Insight Outsight, Mejoder Golpo, Mysteries of Suborno Deb Barman* and *Chhondo Hole Mondo Ki.*

www.ingramcontent.com/pod-product-compliance
Lightning Source LLC
LaVergne TN
LVHW041700070526
838199LV00045B/1136